The rain started suddenly. Not the gentle drops Shade knew from summer showers, but icy driving needles. They dazzled Shade's echo vision, flaring in his mind's eye like shooting stars. He shook his head, trying to clear it.

"Don't let it throw you off," Ariel told him. "Stick close to me. Feels like a storm coming."

The wind screamed around them, and Shade lurched.

"Cling to me, Shade," his mother called out. "It's too rough."

"No!" he snapped. He would not, could not, sink his claws into his mother's fur and cling to her while she flew for both of them. Like he was just a furless pup again.

A savage gust of wind knocked him over onto his back, and his wings buckled.

"Shade!"

"Mom, help!" The wind whipped the words from his mouth. He had no idea where he was, how high he was off the ground. For a split second the fog opened and he caught a glimpse of his mother and the other bats—so far away, how had they gotten so far away?—and then the fog closed up and he was tumbling again.

# SILVERWING

BY
# KENNETH OPPEL

**ALADDIN PAPERBACKS**

I would like to thank my editors,
Marie Campbell and David Gale,
for helping *Silverwing* take flight on the page.

First Aladdin Paperbacks edition May 1999
Copyright © 1997 by Kenneth Oppel

Aladdin Paperbacks
An imprint of Simon & Schuster
Children's Publishing Division
1230 Avenue of the Americas
New York, NY 10020

Also available in a Simon & Schuster Books for
Young Readers hardcover edition.
The text for this book was set in 10-point Stone Serif
Printed and bound in the United States of America
10 9 8

The Library of Congress has cataloged the hardcover edition as follows:
Oppel, Kenneth.
Silverwing / Kenneth Oppel
p.    cm.
Summary: When a newborn bat named Shade but sometimes called
"Runt" becomes separated from his colony during migration,
he grows in ways that prepare him for even greater journeys.
ISBN 0-689-81529-8 (hc.)
1. Bats—Migration—Juvenile fiction. [1. Bats—Migration—Fiction.
2. Growth—Fiction.] I. Title.
PZ10.30555Si    1997    [Fic]—dc21    97-10977
CIP    AC
ISBN 0-689-82558-7 (pbk.)

For Sophia

# PART ONE

# SHADE

Skimming over the banks of the stream, Shade heard the beetle warming up its wings. He flapped harder, picking up speed as he homed in on the musical whine. He was almost invisible against the night sky, the streaks of silver in his thick black fur flashing in the moon's glow.

Airborne now, the beetle was a whirl of shell and wing. Shade still couldn't see it with his eyes—but he could see it with his ears. Caught in his echo vision, the insect hummed and glowed in his mind like a shadow edged in quicksilver. The air whistled in his flared ears as he swooped down. Braking sharply, he scooped the beetle up with his tail membrane, flicked it into his left wing, and volleyed it straight into his open mouth. He veered up and away, and cracked the hard shell with his teeth, savoring the delicious beetle meat as it squirted down his throat. After a few good chomps, he swallowed it whole. Very tasty. Beetles were far and away the best food in the forest. Mealworms and midges weren't bad either. Mosquitoes didn't really taste like much—gauzy, a little prickly at times—but they were also the easiest to catch. He'd already eaten over six hundred this evening, something like that anyway, he'd lost count. They were so slow and clumsy all you had to do was keep your mouth open and swallow every once in a while.

He spun out a web of sound, searching for insects. He was starting to feel full, but he knew he should be eating more. His mother had told him (she'd been telling him for the past ten nights) he had to get fat, because winter was coming. Shade grimaced as he snatched a mealworm from a leaf and gulped. As if he could ever be fat! He knew, though, that there was a long journey ahead of him, south to Hibernaculum where the whole colony would spend the winter.

All around him in the crisp autumn night, he could hear and see other Silverwings streaking through the forest, hunting. Shade stretched his wings luxuriously, only wishing they were longer, more powerful. For a moment he closed his eyes, sailing by sound alone, feeling the air caress the fur of his face and stomach.

His ears pricked suddenly. It was the telltale drumming of a tiger moth in flight. He tilted his right wing and wheeled, locking onto his prey. If he could just catch one—everyone knew how hard they were to catch—and then he'd have a story of his own to tell back at Tree Haven at sunrise.

There it was, chopping its gossamer wings, rocking clumsily. It was laughable, really. He was almost upon it, and maybe this wasn't so hard after all. He cast a net of sound around it and drew in his wings for the plunge. But a hailstorm of noise tore apart his echo vision, and in his mind's eye, he suddenly saw not one but a dozen silvery tiger moths, all veering in different directions.

Shade blinked in confusion. The moth was still in front of him—he could see it with his eyes. Somehow it was scrambling up his echoes with its own. Use your eyes, just your eyes now, he told himself. He flapped harder, coming in fast, claws extended. Wings billowing, he pulled back, and scooped his tail forward to catch his prize when—

The tiger moth simply folded shut its wings and dropped straight down out of his path.

Shade was going too fast, and he couldn't stop. His tail just swept right round underneath him, and he flipped. Clawing air, he plummeted for a split second before righting himself. He cast around for the tiger moth in amazement.

Above him it fluttered along placidly.

"Oh, no you don't!"

He beat his wings and climbed swiftly, gaining. But another bat suddenly flashed in front of him, snapping the tiger moth into his mouth.

"Hey!" cried Shade. "That was mine!"

"You had your chance," said the other bat, and Shade recognized his voice instantly. Chinook. One of the other newborns in the colony.

"I had it," Shade insisted.

"Doubt it." Chinook chewed vigorously and let the wings flutter from his teeth. "This is fabulous, by the way." He made exaggerated smacking sounds. "Well, maybe you'll get lucky one of these nights, Runt."

Shade heard laughter and saw that there was an audience, other newborns fluttering down to roost on a nearby branch. Just wonderful, he thought, everyone will be talking about this for the next two nights.

Flaring his impressive wings, Chinook made a graceful landing, planting both rear claws on the branch and swinging upside down. Shade watched him with a mixture of envy and rage as the others shifted to give him space. There was Jarod, who was never more than a wingbeat from Chinook; he'd fly above the tree line in a lightning storm if Chinook told him to. And there was Yara and Osric and Penumbra. They were always together. Shade didn't want to join them, but flying away now seemed like even more of a defeat. He settled on the branch, a little ways off. His right forearm smarted from his midair flip.

Runt. He hated that name—even though he knew it was true. Compared to Chinook and some of the other newborns, he was small, very small. He'd been born early. Mom wasn't even sure he would survive—that's what she told him later. As a baby he was tiny and furless, floppy skinned, and so weak he could barely cling to her fur. She'd carried him everywhere, even when she went out hunting. When Shade's feeble claws began to falter, she would keep hold of him gently with her own.

Drinking her milk, he'd gradually grown stronger. Within a few weeks, he could even eat some of the mulched-up bugs she caught. His fur started to grow, sleek and black. He gained weight, not a lot, but enough. And everyone in the nursery roost was surprised when he took his first leap, and stayed aloft, wings churning for a few whole seconds before having to make a clumsy and inglorious landing on his chin. He would live after all.

But all the others in the nursery colony were growing faster than him, even the females, with deeper chests, broader wings, and stronger arms to power them. Chinook was considered the most promising newborn, a skilled flyer and hunter. Shade would have given anything for Chinook's body—he certainly didn't want his brain, which was about as active and useful as a pebble.

"Chinook, that was incredible," Jarod said enthusiastically. "The way you just swooped down on that moth—amazing!"

"That was number two tonight."

"Two?" said Jarod. "No! You got two tonight? That's . . ." His admiration seemed boundless. "Incredible!"

Shade ground his teeth as the others muttered their agreement.

Chinook sniffed disdainfully. "I'd have caught more if the hunting was better. It's better in the south. I can hardly wait to get there."

"Oh, sure," agreed Jarod, nodding furiously. "Of course it's better in the south. It's amazing you can get anything to eat up here at all. I can't wait to get down there too."

"My mother says we're leaving in three nights,"

Chinook went on. "And when we get to Hiba—Hiber—"

"Hibernaculum," murmured Shade.

"Yeah," said Chinook, not even glancing at him. It was as if he wasn't even there. Shade was used to being ignored. He wondered why he bothered talking at all. He hated having to watch Chinook hold forth and act like a king.

"So when we get to this place," Chinook went on, "we sleep in these really deep caves with these huge icicles hanging from the roof."

"Stalactites," said Shade. He'd asked his mother about it. "They're not icicles, they're made of minerals dripping from the ceiling. It's not frozen water."

Chinook ignored him, and kept talking about the icicles in the caves. Shade grimaced. Chinook wasn't even interested enough to get things right. He had no curiosity. Shade doubted he'd even seen ice. Shade had, for the first time just last night. Close to dawn, in the creek where they drank, he'd noticed a translucent skin on the water, spreading out from the bank. He couldn't resist testing it, making a low pass, and smacking it with his rear claws. On the second try he felt the ice give way with a satisfying crackle. He'd noticed the other signs of winter coming over the past weeks: the changing brightness of the falling leaves, the sharpness of the air. But the ice was what made him realize winter really was coming, and it made him anxious.

He didn't like to think about the coming migration. Hibernaculum was millions of wingbeats away, and he harbored a secret fear he wasn't strong enough to make it. And his mother must have been worried too, or she wouldn't be telling him to eat all the time. And even if he got there, the idea of sleeping for four months filled him with dread. They wouldn't be feeding at all through the winter, just sleeping, their bodies glinting with frost. And what if he couldn't sleep? What if he just hung there in the cave, with everyone else fast asleep around him? It was a stupid idea anyway, sleeping for so long. Such a waste! Maybe other bats could sleep that long, but he knew he couldn't. It just wasn't possible. Sometimes he found it hard enough sleeping through even a single day. There was so much he needed to do: practice flying, learn how to land better, hunt better, catch a tiger moth. He needed to get bigger and stronger, and he didn't see how he was expected to do all that while sleeping away the winter.

"I can't wait to meet my father," Chinook was saying.

"Me either," Rasha agreed.

And then everyone was talking about fathers, repeating stories from their mothers and sisters. At the moment the Silverwings were split in half. Tree Haven was a nursery colony, where the females reared the newborns. Farther to the southeast, the males spent the summer at Stone Hold. But once the migration started, they'd rendezvous and make the long journey south to Hibernaculum together.

Shade listened silently, feeling his face harden, wishing they'd all just shut up.

"My father's huge," Chinook was saying over the others. Chinook never waited for anyone to finish talking. He just barged right in and everyone always stopped to listen. Shade couldn't understand why: The only things Chinook ever talked about were how much he'd eaten or which of his muscles was sorest from his latest heroic feat.

"My father's wings," he told them now, "go from here to that tree over there, and he can eat ten thousand bugs in one night, and he's faster than anyone else in the colony. And once he fought with an owl and killed it."

"No bat can kill an owl," Shade snapped. It was the first thing he'd said in a while, and the anger in his voice surprised him.

"My father did."

"They're too big." He knew Chinook was just boasting, but he couldn't let it go.

"A strong bat can do it, easy."

"No chance."

"You don't know everything, Runt. You calling me a liar?"

Shade felt his fur bristle in defiance. He knew he was being taunted, and he knew he was about to say yes, yes, you are a liar. The words were snagged in his throat like dry shells.

But a few sharp notes of birdsong carried through the forest, and they all stiffened.

"There's the dawn chorus," said Penumbra unnecessarily. Everyone knew what it was. "I guess we should head back."

Chinook and the other newborns rustled their wings in agreement, ready for flight.

"Yeah, go ahead," said Shade with a casual yawn, "I'm just going to take a peek at the sun."

Their reaction was so satisfying, he had to wrinkle his nostrils to keep from smiling. They all stared at him in silence, the fur between their eyes ridged with consternation.

"What're you talking about?" Chinook scoffed.

"You can't look at the sun," said Yara, shaking her head.

"Well, I thought I'd give it a try."

It was the first and most important thing all newborns were told. There were other rules—too many, as far as Shade was concerned—but this was the one they were taught most fiercely. You must *never* look at the sun. It was as simple and final as that.

"It'll blind you," said Jarod. "Burn your eyeballs right out of your head."

"Then turn you to dust," Osric added, not without relish.

Shade shrugged with regal indifference.

"And there're the owls," said Penumbra fretfully. She looked around. "We should get going."

In the distance Shade could hear the mothers calling

their children back to Tree Haven. And then his mother, Ariel's, unmistakable voice: "Shade . . . Shade . . ." He felt a quick tug at his heart. She would worry. And he was already in trouble from a few nights ago when he landed on the ground (breaking another rule) just to get a closer look at a glistening spider's web. Just for a few seconds, but he'd been caught, and scolded ferociously in front of the other newborns.

"Just a quick peek," he told the others, glancing at the brightening sky. "Won't be long."

"You're so weird," said Osric, but there it was, that look Shade had been craving, a look of grudging admiration.

"He's not going to see the sun," said Chinook irritably. "He's just saying that."

"I'll tell you about it when I get back to Tree Haven," said Shade breezily. "Unless you want to come, Chinook."

It was a delicious moment of silence as Jarod, Penumbra, Yara, and Osric all looked expectantly at their hero. A challenge had been issued, and Chinook knew it. He gouged one of his claws into the bark.

"Well, never mind," said Shade cheerfully, ready to light from the branch.

"Wait! I'm coming," said Chinook, and then, more fiercely, "I'm coming with you."

"I know this is just some stupid game," said Chinook as they flew through the forest, away from Tree Haven. "We'll see who backs down first."

Shade had to push himself to keep up, and it irritated him. He was always having to flap harder, try harder, so he wouldn't fall behind. He hated the easy pump of Chinook's wings, but watched carefully, trying to copy it.

"We'll go to the top of the hill," he said, hoping he didn't sound out of breath. "We'll see the sun quicker there. What d'you think?"

Chinook just grunted distractedly, then said, "What about the owls?"

Was that a note of worry in his voice? Shade felt encouraged.

"Just stick close to the trees, they won't even see us."

Another grunt.

Shade could see birds beginning to stir in their nests and on their perches, joining in on the dawn chorus, puffing out their feathers. Sleeping birds were such a normal part of his nighttime world, but he'd never seen many awake, and now a few sang out in surprise as he and Chinook darted past.

They reached the summit and roosted at the tip of the highest tree, pressed close against the trunk for cover. The long valley curved before them, an unbroken canopy of trees except for the one dusty Human road cutting through. He'd never seen anything on it, not a Human, not one of their noisy vehicles. They were a long way away from most things, his mother always said.

The dawn chorus was building now, rising up all around them.

"What d'you want to see the sun for anyway?"

"I just want to see it."

"What for?"

"I'm curious. Aren't you?"

A slight pause. "No." Another pause. "What if it turns us to dust?"

"It doesn't turn anything else to dust."

He was enjoying this: Chinook was actually listening to him for a change; it was almost as if he needed reassurance.

"My mother told a story about a bat. All his wings and bones and teeth, just a pile of dust."

"Just a story."

But he felt a twist of fear in his stomach.

"Let's go back," said Chinook after a moment. "We can tell the others we saw it. We'll keep it secret, okay?"

Shade considered this. Here was Chinook, asking him for something. It was certainly pleasant, this feeling of power.

"Go ahead," said Shade. He would not leave. He wanted his victory without any compromise.

The sky was very bright in the east now, brighter than he'd ever seen it. He squinted with the faint whiskery pain behind his eyes. What if the stories were right? What if it did blind him?

"Not much longer," he muttered.

Chinook shifted on the branch, wings rustling against the bark.

"Shhh," Shade hissed at him. "Over there." He tilted his chin.

An owl sat stone still in a nearby tree, half hidden behind a screen of leaves.

"Not afraid are you?" he whispered at Chinook. "A strong bat has nothing to be afraid of."

Shade was afraid, but he didn't think the owl had seen them. Even if it had, he knew it wasn't allowed to attack them until the sun had risen. It was the law. He doubted Chinook knew this, though, since it wasn't the kind of thing mothers told the newborns. The only reason he knew was he'd overheard his own mother talking with some of the colony elders when she thought he was asleep. It was about the only good thing about being a runt: When he was younger he'd been carried everywhere with her, even to special meetings for the adults. He'd picked up a lot of things that way.

A dreadful hooting noise emanated from the owl's throat, making Shade's fur lift. Then, with a flurry, the owl lit from the branch and flew away across the sky, its wings pumping silently.

Shade let out his breath.

"I—I can't," said Chinook, and he dropped from the branch, pounding his way fast toward Tree Haven. Shade watched him disappear into the foliage. He felt strangely disappointed, and didn't know why.

He could go now too.

He'd won.

But it wasn't enough. He wanted something more, and it surprised him. He genuinely wanted to see the sun. This thing that they were absolutely forbidden.

Across the valley a band of white light spread from the tree line. He was surprised how long this was all taking. Half the sky was already pale gray, and still no sun? What was it doing?

He blinked, turned away, and found himself staring straight at a wall of dense feathers. He looked up into the huge hooded eyes of an owl, perched at the end of his branch. Without a sound Shade pressed himself deep against the bark, but he knew he'd been spotted. They were so quiet, an owl's wings. They could sneak up on you. The owl's eyes held on him, and then the massive horned head swiveled eerily to the bright horizon, checking for the sun. Shade let his echo vision creep across the owl, taking a good long look: the thick feathers cloaking ferocious strength, the wickedly hooked beak that could rip through flesh in a second. And he knew it didn't even need its eyes to see him. Like him, all owls had echo vision too.

He stared, hating the owl. No bat could kill an owl. They were giants, five times as big, maybe more. He should have been more afraid. He was smaller, but he could go places it couldn't, between tight gaps in branches; he could fold himself into a crevice in a tree's trunk; he could make himself almost invisible against bark.

There was a sudden rush of air behind him and there was his mother, hovering.

"Fly!" she hissed. "Now!"

Her voice was so urgent and so angry he followed her instantly. Down the hill they plunged, hugging the tree line. He looked back over his wing and saw the owl, following at a distance, its gigantic wings swinging leisurely. The sun had not yet broken the horizon.

They flew over the creek and the owl was still there.

Shade felt a sudden warmth on his wings, and looked. They shone brightly. The sun.

"Into the trees!" Ariel cried over her wing. "Don't look back!"

He looked.

A tiny sliver of the sun had cleared the horizon, spilling dazzling light into the valley. It was so powerful, so intense it sucked the breath right out of him, and he had to close his eyes tight.

He locked onto his mother with his echo vision, and followed her as she plunged below the tree line. The rank smell of the owl crashed over him as its claws whistled past his tail, nearly piercing his wings.

He was down among the trees now, and all around him, the birds were rising and setting up a terrible shriek. Weaving crazily through the foliage, he pushed himself hard to keep up with his mother. At last, they burst out into the clearing. But so did the owl, who'd been following from above the trees. It dropped toward them like a hailstone. Shade and his mother rolled in opposite directions to avoid its claws, then came together again, streaking toward the mighty gnarled branches of Tree Haven, through the knothole and into the safe darkness inside.

# TREE HAVEN

Tree Haven was a vast, ancient oak, with furrowed bark, and thick, gnarled roots buckling from the ground. Hundreds of years ago it had been struck by lightning, killing the tree and petrifying the outside. The Silverwings had hollowed out the great trunk, and the many branches, and used it as a nursery colony ever since. Every spring the females returned to give birth and rear their young. It was perfect. There were only a handful of openings, well-hidden knotholes, through which the bats flew every dawn and dusk. No birds or beasts could work their way inside. The bats made their roosts on the mossy inner walls, in crevices and ledges and hollows, and inside the multitude of branches snaking from the trunk.

As Shade burst through the knothole with his mother, the bats roosting around the entrance looked over fearfully. Outside, the owl screamed again in fury as it battered the tree with its claws, once, twice, before flying off, hooting balefully. As he made a quick landing beside his mother, Shade heard the flurry of questions over his racing heart.

"What happened?" and "Why were you out so late?" and "Didn't you hear the dawn chorus?" and "How did you escape the owl?"

Ariel ignored them and turned urgently to Shade.

"Are you hurt?"

"Don't think so—"

She inspected his wings and tail anyway, roughly nosing his ribs and stomach to make sure nothing was broken, nothing cut. Then she folded her wings around him and held him tight for a long time. He realized she was trembling and when she pulled back, her eyes shone with anger.

"Why did you do that?"

Shade looked away. He was aware of the other bats nearby, felt the fur burn across his face. He spoke quietly. "Chinook was being . . . he was saying things about owls and how his father fought one, and I just wanted to do something—" He was about to say *brave*, but she cut him off.

"It was a childish thing, a dangerous thing." She made no attempt to lower her voice. "You could've been killed, like that." She flicked the tip of her wing so it made a sharp, final snap in the air. "And Chinook with you."

"How'd you know about Chinook?"

"I ran into him while looking for you."

"He told, then," Shade scoffed.

"Lucky for you he did." She stared at him. "It was foolishness like this that got your father killed."

Shade couldn't speak for a moment. "He wanted to see the sun?" he asked urgently.

She'd never told him this. All he knew about his father's death was that, last spring, he was out one night, too far from the roost, too late, and an owl hunted him down in the dawn's light and killed him. His father's name was Cassiel.

Ariel nodded, suddenly weary. "Yes. He was always talking about it. Because he was curious—no, because he was headstrong, because he wouldn't think." All her anger surged back. "That's not going to happen to you. I won't lose both my mate and my son in one year. I won't stand for it."

"Why didn't you tell me?" He felt abruptly resentful.

"I didn't want to give you ideas. You've got enough of those as it is." She sighed, and her eyes lost their fierceness. "You sure you're all right?"

"Why'd he want to see the sun?"

"Promise me you'll never do that again."

"Did you make my father promise?"

"Will you promise me?" she insisted.

"It's not right," said Shade, frowning. "I mean that the owls don't let us see the sun. Do you think it's fair, Mom?"

She gave an exasperated sigh, and closed her eyes for a moment. "It has nothing to do with fair or right or wrong. It's just the way things . . ." she broke off in annoyance. "I'm not going to argue with you. You do as I say, it's as simple as that. You don't know the trouble you've caused, for all of us."

"But why, we got away, we—"

But he didn't finish because Mercury, the messenger for the colony elders, was making a slow spiral down the trunk toward them.

"You're both all right?" he asked as he settled gracefully beside them.

"Yes."

"The elders are anxious to speak with you. Are you strong enough to go to the upper roost, or shall I ask them to come see you here?"

"No, I can go. Stay here," Ariel told Shade.

"They asked you to bring your son."

Shade shared a quick look with his mother. He'd been in trouble before, plenty of times. But this was the first time he'd been summoned before the elders. Mercury launched himself back into the air and Shade followed after Ariel, back up the trunk. He sensed the gaze of a hundred bats as he ascended, and felt acutely self-conscious, but pleasantly flushed. Usually nobody even gave him a second glance. Now he was important enough to be called before the elders. He let his eyes boldly pass over the curious faces of the roosting onlookers. And there was Chinook beside his mother, but he looked away before Shade could shoot him a smirk of triumph.

"You've got nothing to grin about," Ariel snapped. "Hurry up."

They'd passed countless passageways and were nearing the upper reaches of the tree now, and Shade felt a queasy twisting in his stomach. He had never been this high. The central trunk came to a blunt end, but Mercury led them into a branch that veered straight upward, kinking and curving as it reached into the sky.

At the branch's peak hung the four colony elders, quietly speaking among themselves as Shade and his mother found roosts beneath them. Mercury fluttered to Frieda and whispered in her ear before retreating to a small crevice in the shadows of the chamber, ready if called upon.

Aurora, Bathsheba, Lucretia, and Frieda: Shade knew the names of the elders, but he had never spoken to them. He saw them only from a distance, and they filled him with a kind of awe. They were all old bats, well beyond childbearing, and it was strange for Shade to see females in the roost without newborns nearby. Frieda was the oldest of the four and to Shade the most mysterious. Her actual age wasn't known, but no one could remember a time when she hadn't been chief elder of the Silverwing colony. Her wings were creased, but still supple and strong, and her claws were gnarled like the roots of an old tree, but wickedly sharp. According to Shade's mother, Frieda was still a fierce hunter. The fur around her face was shot through with more gray than silver or black now, and there were a few mangy patches on her body, which were probably just signs of age, but Shade liked to think at least some of them were old battle scars.

The most mysterious thing about Frieda was the small metal band around her left forearm. No other bat in the colony had one. Shade asked his mother about it frequently, but she just shook her head, and told him she didn't know where it came from or how Frieda got it. The other newborns were just as hopeless. There were a few halfhearted suggestions, but—and this was always infuriating to Shade—no one seemed very curious or interested: Frieda had a band, and as far as they were concerned, that was that.

"You made a close escape by the sounds of it," Frieda said to them now. "But why were you out so late, Ariel? What happened?"

"I was looking for Shade."

"Was he lost?" This was Bathsheba, and her harsh voice put Shade on edge.

"No," said Ariel. "He made a foolish dare with Chinook. They were waiting for the sun to rise."

"Where is Chinook?" asked Frieda.

"He's safe. He had the sense to return to Tree Haven before sunrise."

Shade frowned, and had to clamp down on his mouth to keep quiet. The *sense*? Chinook got scared, he flew off like a frightened moth!

"Yet your son stayed," said Frieda, staring so intently at Shade that he had to look at his feet.

"Yes, and I found him just in time. An owl was waiting in the tree, ready to take him."

"But the sun rose before you reached Tree Haven," said Bathsheba pointedly.

"Yes," Ariel replied sadly.

There was a brief, terrible silence in the elders' roost. And when Bathsheba next spoke, Shade could not believe what he heard.

"Then you should have left your son for the owl."

"I know," Ariel said.

Shade looked at her in horror.

"It is the law," Bathsheba persisted.

"I know the law."

"Then why did you break it?"

Shade saw the anger flare again in his mother's eyes. "I did what any mother would have done."

The betrayal Shade had felt only seconds ago was washed away in a swell of pride and love for his mother. Bathsheba began an angry reply to this, but with a gentle *whoosh*, Frieda spread her wings wide and the other bat fell silent.

"We know what you suffered in the spring, Ariel. And how bravely you've dealt with the loss of Cassiel. And you're right. What you did was only natural. But the law is not natural; it is cruel."

Bathsheba chittered impatiently. "Everyone was saddened by the death of Cassiel. But Ariel isn't the only one to lose a mate. Many of us have. You say the law is cruel, Frieda, but it can help us too. The law keeps us safe at night, not by day. If we are obedient, we can at least avoid some of these needless deaths." She directed her hard eyes at Ariel again. "Your actions were selfish, and you've put the whole roost in danger."

Frieda sighed. "This, I'm afraid, may very well be true."

"Terrible as it is," Bathsheba continued coldly, "if you'd left your son, the owls would have taken him, and this would be over. Now they will feel cheated; they will want justice."

Ariel nodded. "Yes, I know this is my fault."

"No," Shade blurted before he could stop himself. He hated the resignation in his mother's voice, hated the way Bathsheba glowered down at her. How dare she talk to his mother like this! Every set of eyes was on him now, and he felt all the thoughts in his head whirl uselessly. "I mean, it's my fault," he hurried on. "I'm the—it was me who wanted to see the sun, I talked Chinook into it, but really the sun hardly came up at all, so I don't see why the owls were so upset. I'm sorry I've caused this trouble, and I don't know much about the law, but I think it's cruel and unfair, just like Frieda said."

In the following silence Shade wished, for the first time in his life, that he could be even smaller than he was, so small he would just blink out altogether.

"You've obviously coddled your boy," Bathsheba said frostily to Ariel, "and made him headstrong and insolent. Didn't you tell him how dangerous the sun was?"

"It didn't turn me to dust," Shade mumbled. He couldn't believe he'd done it again, the words just sliding out.

"What?" Bathsheba said.

"Or blind me," Shade muttered. "The sun. Those were just stories."

"That's enough, Shade," his mother said sharply. "I plan to punish him," she told Bathsheba.

Bathsheba snorted, unimpressed. "Little good that will do if the owls demand compensation."

"We'll worry about that later," said Frieda sternly. "The boy only did what many of you would have liked to—or maybe you've forgotten that. He is young and foolish, yes, but don't be so quick to judge him. Thank you, Ariel. Shade. Rest well."

Frieda turned her piercing gaze on him once again, and Shade felt strangely illuminated by it. He looked back into the old bat's dark eyes for only a moment (which was as much as he could endure) before humbly bowing his head and muttering his good-byes.

By the time Shade and his mother left the elders' roost, most of the colony was already asleep, hanging from their roosts, the newborns pressed close against their mothers, enfolded in their wings.

"Wash up," his mother told him when they'd settled back at their roost.

Shade started licking the dust and grit from his wings. The owl already seemed like such a long time ago, but he conjured up the silent pounding of its wings, the quick whistle of its flashing claws.

"We made a pretty great escape, didn't we?" he said.

"Thrilling," said his mother tersely.

"I really did see the sun, you know."

She nodded curtly.

"Aren't you interested?"

"No."

"Are you still angry with me?"

"No. But I don't want you to be like your father."

"Not much chance of that," Shade grimaced. "He was a big bat, right?"

"Yes. He was a big bat. But you might be too, one day."

"Might." It wasn't very satisfying. He looked up from his licking. "Mom, a bat can't kill an owl, can he?"

"No," she said. "No bat can."

"Right," said Shade sadly. "They're too big. There's no way any bat could do it."

"Forget what Chinook said."

"Yeah," said Shade.

"Here, you've got a big dirty patch." She came closer and began pulling her claws gently through the fur of his back.

"I can do it," said Shade, but only halfheartedly. He relaxed his aching shoulders as his mother combed through his fur again and again. A wonderful floating feeling lulled him, and he felt safe and warm and happy, and wished he could always be like this. But as he closed his eyes, the image of the rising sun, that dazzling sliver of light, still burned on the back of his eyelids.

Shade tried to feel sorry for what he'd done, but it wasn't easy, especially when he realized he was famous, at least to the newborns. The very next evening, Osric, Yara, Penumbra, and several others demanded a full retelling of his adventure with the owl, and he was only too happy to oblige, mostly sticking to the truth, but occasionally juicing it up with a few made-up details. Chinook stayed away, and Jarod too. But Shade knew it would all get back to them.

He didn't have long to revel in his new fame, though, because soon the roost emptied as all the bats left for the night's hunting, and Shade had to stay behind. This was part of his punishment: He was grounded. He had to stay in Tree Haven all night with the old, boring bats who were too feeble to do much hunting, and preferred it inside anyway. For one hour at midnight he'd be allowed out to feed. But even then his mother would be right beside him, and he couldn't stray out of sight of the roost. He wasn't too upset by this, since he knew they'd be leaving Tree Haven on their journey in two nights anyway, and his punishment would then be over.

Still, he wasn't going to let the time go to waste. Inside the trunk he practiced his take-offs and landings; he targeted twigs or bits of moss with his echo vision, pretending they were tiger moths, and dove in for the kill. And all the while he was thinking. About the sun, about the owls. And he thought about his father, who like him, had wanted to see the sun.

Over the months he'd practically deafened his mother with questions about Cassiel, how he looked, what he was like. But try as he might he'd never been able to feel a connection with him. Now though, knowing about how he died, he felt a frail spider's thread running between them. He was just a runt, but he'd wanted to see the sun, just like his father.

He was catching his breath after a spectacular dive-bomb when he felt a rush of air around him, and looked to see Frieda settling beside him.

"Tell me about the sun," she said.

His tongue felt too heavy. The chief elder of the colony stared with those piercing eyes. Her wings creaked as she folded them against her body, and he was aware of a slightly musty odor rising off her, the smell of age, he supposed. But she smiled at him, and her face wrinkled at the eyes, and Shade felt less nervous.

"Well, I saw it," he began hesitantly, and then stumbled on and told her everything he could remember. It wasn't much, but he was eager to tell it, delighted really. His mother certainly didn't care. Frieda listened carefully, nodding now and then.

"You've seen it too, haven't you?" he asked impulsively.

"You're right, I have. A long time ago."

"It's round, isn't it, like the moon?"

"Yes. But bigger."

He shook his head in amazement. He couldn't even imagine the brightness of it.

"You just wanted to see it, then? Like me?" he asked Frieda.

She nodded. "When I was younger, a lot of us did. Some were willing to die for it. Not like now. They don't care. They might think the law is unfair, but they aren't willing to fight it. Like Bathsheba. And in many ways they're wise. Look at your father, look what almost happened to you and Ariel."

"How come we're not allowed to see it? I mean, I know it's the law, but why?"

"We're banished creatures, Shade, and have been for millions of years."

"Banished?"

"Punished, sent away."

"For what? What did we do?"

"It's easier if you hear for yourself. Come with me."

# THE ECHO CHAMBER

Last dawn Shade had traveled to the summit of Tree Haven, and now Frieda was leading him to its very depths. They spiraled down the length of the great trunk, and Shade again marveled at the sheer size of the tree. Down and down until they landed on the mossy bottom. He was aware of how much cooler it was, and the strong smell of soil and wood. He thought he'd explored every winding inch of Tree Haven, every passageway and hollow, but he'd never noticed this small archway of gnarled wood, which Frieda was scuttling toward on all fours.

He followed her through, and down, and instantly he knew he was beneath the earth. His echoes bounced harshly against the walls of the narrow passageway.

"Here we are," said Frieda up ahead.

The floor of the tunnel fell away, and Shade gladly opened his wings and swooped down into a large cave. He felt the cold seeping through the stone walls and thought: winter. And then he heard the wind—or at least he thought it was wind. But as he flared his ears, listened harder, he realized it was voices he was hearing, bat voices, so many of them, mumbling, mumbling, over one another, like a ghostly breeze through leaves. It made the flesh beneath his fur crawl.

"Who's down there?" he asked, faltering.

"Nobody," said Frieda. "I'll show you."

"There're voices . . ."

"You'll see. This way."

Frieda led him deeper still, down to the bottom of the cave, and then landed on a narrow ledge. In a small niche in the rough stone Shade saw a panel of mud and mulched-up leaves. The voices were coming from behind it.

"Quickly now," Frieda told him, and pushed through the soft center of the panel with her nose.

He didn't know what to expect. Maybe a mournful chorus of ghosts, maybe only one with a thousand weeping mouths. He found himself in a surprisingly small, completely round, and totally deserted cave. But it wasn't truly deserted. All around him, like currents of warm air, were voices, moaning at his ears, getting caught in his fur, his wings.

"Fold your wings tight," Frieda said, carefully closing the mud panel behind Shade, "and stay still."

He barely breathed. Still the voices seemed faint and far away, but he could hear them more clearly now as they swirled about:

". . . in the winter of that year . . ."

". . . owls took their revenge . . ."

". . . fifteen newborns died in the nursery . . ."

". . . rebellion crushed after the battle . . ."

And he realized they were echoes, bouncing off the walls of the cave, again and again and again.

"See how smooth the walls are," Frieda whispered. "It took years to hollow them out, polish them. Generations. But it had to be smooth, or else the echoes would snag and fade. Here they can bounce for centuries. It's not perfect. Sound escapes even through the door they so carefully built, and which I tend to every spring. Sound gets old, loses its power."

"What's it for?" Shade asked.

"This is the history of the Silverwing colony,"

explained Frieda. "Right here. Every year one of the elders is appointed to sing the year's stories to the walls, and there they stay."

"How do you keep them all straight?" Shade wanted to know, his ears flicking from one eddy of sound to the next. His mind felt cluttered and confused.

"It takes a certain talent," said Frieda. "Concentration, patience. Few can do it, but I have a feeling about you . . . here, let me help." Shade watched as the old bat swiveled her ears, eyes darting as if in search of insects. "Yes, here it is, the oldest story of all . . . catch it now . . . concentrate . . ."

Shade moved his head up against Frieda's, eyes closed, ears pricked high, and suddenly there was a voice inside his head, so clear, so much a part of him, that he jerked back and pinned his ears flat to escape it.

"It's an odd feeling, isn't it," said Frieda.

"It gets right inside you," he said sheepishly.

"It's all right. Try again."

He tensed as the sound flowed into him, but this time held on.

"Long ago," came the voice, "millions and millions of years ago, the world was an empty place." It was a female's voice, steady and melodious, and it gave Shade the strangest feeling to think she had spoken these words so long ago, and he was hearing them now, as if for the first time. He listened intently, eyes clamped shut.

"There was only Nocturna, the Winged Spirit, whose wings spanned the entire night sky, and *were* the night sky, and contained the stars and the moon and the wind. One by one Nocturna fashioned creatures . . ."

The words faded away, and without warning, his mind was filled with pictures. A brilliant silvery world flared up before him, as clear as his own echo vision at night.

His eyes popped open in surprise.

"What's happening?"

"Echo pictures," the elder told him patiently. "We see

with echoes, and with practice it's also possible to sing echo pictures into bats' heads."

"It's so real!"

"Listen. You'll lose it if you're not careful."

He shut his eyes, exhaled slowly, and let the silvery world fill his mind once again.

The beginning of the world—and he was there, watching it.

He soared past a thousand different birds, skimmed over a thousand different beasts on the ground. The earth steamed. He could almost feel the heat, the newness of things.

He saw bats, lifting from trees, beating their way through the air.

And it was full daylight.

The sun burned high in the sky.

"We were allowed then," he muttered, incredulous. "We were allowed to see the sun!"

The scene changed abruptly, and he was at the top of a giant tree, and all around him raged a huge battle. Birds dived down at beasts, fighting with their claws and beaks, carrying their smaller victims away and dropping them to their deaths. But the beasts fought back, leaping up and snapping the birds in their jaws, smashing them with taloned claws. The beasts scaled the trees, destroying nests, pouncing on birds in the branches.

Shade looked down with horror and saw a wildcat scrabbling up his own tree toward him, and he cried out in alarm.

But at that moment he was suddenly higher in the sky, overseeing things from a great, safe distance.

"A war!" Shade called out excitedly to Frieda, his eyes still closed, still watching.

"The Great Battle of the Birds and the Beasts," he heard Frieda say.

"But why?"

"No one knows what started it."

He noticed something. "Where are the bats?"

"We refused to fight. Each side asked us to join them, but we said no."

The silvery images in his head shifted again, and he was flying over a ravaged forest, the trees naked and broken, the earth pockmarked with animal holes and trenches. He knew the battle must have gone on for a long time, years and years.

He soared down over a great field and saw beasts and birds gathered there together, holding some kind of important meeting.

"The peace treaty," he heard Frieda say. She was listening along with him.

The bats were there too, and all the other creatures seemed angry with them, shouting and pointing. A great owl spread its wings in judgment, and a huge wolf threw back his head and howled. The bats flew, spiraling up into the air, spreading across the sky.

And suddenly it was night.

"What happened?" Shade cried.

"The beasts blamed us for losing the battle; the birds branded us cowards for refusing to fight. Listen."

The voice that Shade heard at the beginning came back into his head now.

"For millions of years we have lived in the dark. The sunlight hurts our eyes now. The Winged Spirit, Nocturna, was angry with the other creatures for banishing us. Though she could not undo what had been done, she gave us new gifts to help us survive: She darkened our fur, so we might blend in with the night; she gave us the echo vision, so we could hunt in the dark. But the greatest gift she gave us was the Promise."

There was a brief silence, and then:

"Long ago, millions and millions of years ago, the world was an empty place . . ."

The message had come full circle, and Shade shifted his head out of the echo stream. He felt as if he'd been away for a long time.

He turned to Frieda. He'd heard of Nocturna before, every newborn had, the mysterious Winged Spirit who made everything. But he'd heard so many new things, and was so knotted up inside with emotion, he scarcely knew where to begin.

"We didn't do anything!" he exclaimed. He'd expected something terrible, some crime that would make him shudder and feel ashamed of his ancestors. "They banished us just because we didn't take sides in the war!"

"To the birds and beasts, we were cowards and traitors."

"But before then we could really fly in the day? Is that true? We were free?"

"I believe so, yes."

"What's the Promise?"

"That's here too," Frieda said, tilting her head around the echo chamber. "Let's see if we can find it. It's one of the oldest here . . ."

Shade knew Frieda could find it in a second, and that she was trying to teach him how to use the echo chamber. Together, they sifted through the eddies of sound, and Shade soon discovered that they were all different. The newer messages were clearer and slightly louder; the older ones had a faint hiss to them, words and pictures occasionally muffled, or obscured altogether.

"You're getting close," Frieda said.

He found one story gusting across the cave's bottom, quite faint. He listened, caught a few words. "Is this it?"

Frieda cocked her head, squinted, and gave a nod. "Well done."

Shade latched onto the echo and let the story fill his head. It was another voice this time, unsteady and old, but filled with a kind of radiant hope.

"This is the story of Nocturna's Promise. It has been carried from bat to bat for over a million years, and I speak it to these walls so that future Silverwing generations will know what has passed, and what will come to pass. The promise was made one day long ago . . ."

Shade was in an ancient forest, peering out over the fields. There were no bats in sight. He was alone in the middle of the day, the sun high in the sky. Suddenly darkness seeped over the earth, as if a giant bat were slowly unfurling her wings and blocking out the light. The beasts shrank back in terror. The birds shrieked and fled to the cover of the trees.

The sun disappeared.

Not disappeared exactly, but to Shade it was as if a huge black eye had opened in front of it. Nocturna's eye. That was the first thought that popped into his head. Only the rim of the sun remained. And he was staring at it.

This blazing ring of silver light.

So bright that even as a picture in his mind, it made his eyes smart.

All at once bats were streaming from their roosts, and he was among them, an ecstasy of wings. They knotted in the sky, then flew apart, swirling beneath this silver ring.

It was the first time in a thousand years they had been out in the day.

The dark sky began to speak, and Shade felt every inch of his body tingle. He knew without a doubt that this was Nocturna's voice, speaking to the bats long ago.

"One day your banishment will end, and the cruel law will be broken. You will no more have to fear the claws of the owls or the jaws of the beasts. And you will be free to return to the light of day once again."

The silver ring in the sky slowly faded, and then black silence filled Shade's head.

The echo began to repeat, and Shade shrugged it off, turning urgently to Frieda.

"Will there be another war? Is that what it means?"

"Maybe. I don't know."

"When? When will it happen?"

The bat elder shook her head. "Maybe not in my lifetime,

or yours." She paused. "But I think it will be sooner than that."

"How come?" Shade asked, startled.

"Because of this," Frieda told him, unfolding her wing and revealing the silver band on her forearm. Shade gasped, as if seeing it for the first time. He remembered the image from the echo story: the sun being blotted out by Nocturna's black eye, so that it was only a blazing ring of light. A ring of silver. Just like the band on Frieda's forearm.

"You see it, don't you?" Frieda asked.

He nodded. "How did you get it?"

"The Humans gave it to me when I was young. Not much older than you, really. There were a couple of us in the forest one night, and they took hold of us and fastened the bands, and let us go. I believe it's a sign, Shade. A sign of the Promise to come. I don't know what part the Humans will play in it, but I believe they've come to help us in some way."

Shade sent a delicate wash of sound over the band, and picked out the Human markings around the rim. He could only wonder at their strangeness, the curves and sharp edges. He'd seen owl scratchings once, and raccoon hieroglyphs, but these were by far the most complicated.

"May I?" he asked.

"Yes, of course," Frieda replied, extending her forearm.

Shade touched the band with the tip of his claw.

"Did the Humans give bands to anyone else?"

"Not for a long time—so long I began to wonder if they meant anything at all. But two winters ago, yes, they came again, and banded some males."

"My father," said Shade instinctively.

"Ariel told you, did she?"

"No. She doesn't talk about him much."

Frieda nodded. "We used to tell all the newborns these stories, the ones you've just heard. That was years ago. But most of the elders thought we should stop. It was no use thinking about the Promise, they said, something that might never come. That's how Bathsheba thinks. They didn't want any more bloodshed. About fifteen years before you were born a rebellion sprung up, but the bats didn't stand a chance against the owls. They fought anyway. We fought, I should say."

"You did?" Shade said, gazing again at the scars on Frieda's body.

"I was lucky to escape with my life. After that, the elders wanted to just stay in the night, and forget they'd ever had the freedom to fly in the day. Most bats think they're right, and I can't fault them for it. It makes sense. But for some bats, they just can't let go of that idea of the sun, of freedom. I'm like that. And your father was too."

"Mom said he was killed by owls."

"He flew off somewhere just a few nights before we started our journey back north. He didn't tell anyone where he was going, at least I never heard of it. Maybe he told one of the others. All I know was there was something he wanted to find out, about the bands, about the Humans, maybe. And he never did come back. There were a couple others before him who disappeared too."

"Mom just said he was foolish for wanting to see the sun."

"I know that she never agreed with his views. And she wants to protect you, Shade. She might not have told you the whole truth, but I suspect there's a lot Cassiel never told her either. Try not to be angry with her."

"We should fight them," Shade said with a cold, sudden fury. How could the other Silverwings be so feeble? Letting the owls and the other birds and beasts tell them what to do for millions of years. What right did they have? "If all the bats would fight then we could—"

But Frieda was shaking her head. "No, not even your father thought that, Shade. He knew we couldn't win in battle, that was obvious. He thought there was something else coming, something we needed."

Shade looked away, ashamed at his outburst. He felt immensely tired, as if he'd lived through all the stories in the echo chamber.

"Why did you show me all this?" he asked. What was the point? he wondered. There was nothing he could do to change the past, bring his father back, or even change the future. He was a newborn runt in a Silverwing colony in the middle of nowhere.

Frieda smiled at him, and he didn't find the deep wrinkles in her face so frightening anymore. "You're not like the others. I see something in you, a kind of brightness I don't want to be smothered. You're curious. You want to know about things. I've been watching you. You're a good listener too: You'll hear things no one else can. And this is far more important than your size, Shade."

He flushed at the compliment, and only wished he could believe it. He had so many more questions he wanted to ask, but there was a fluttering of wings outside the echo chamber and Shade heard Mercury's voice.

"Frieda," the messenger said urgently. "The owls are coming. And they have fire."

# ABLAZE

Shade circled anxiously over the peak of Tree Haven with Frieda and Mercury, watching the owls soar toward them. They flew high up in the sky, thirty-five, maybe forty in an arrowhead formation, and the eerie silence of their powerful wingbeats made Shade feel sick. Clutched in their claws were long thin sticks, the ends glittering like dangerous stars. Fire. Shade stared in horror. Only the owls had fire. Hundreds of years ago they'd stolen some from Humans and kept it burning in secret nests deep in the forest.

"Mercury," Frieda said with amazing calm, "go spread the news through the forest, and tell everyone to take cover there. Tell them there's to be no fighting. Shade, go back inside and make sure everyone is out of the roost."

He swallowed hard.

"Do you understand?" Frieda asked him.

"Yes."

"You know what might happen?"

He nodded fiercely and flew off, grateful to have something to do. He dove back inside Tree Haven, crying out the warning.

"Clear the roost! Clear the roost!"

He poured all his energy into his task, trying not to think of the fire in the owls' claws. He started at the bottom and worked his way up, darting through every twist and turn of the branches to make sure he didn't miss anyone. "Clear the roost! Everyone out!" And all this because of him—his fault. Lucky that most everyone was out hunting; the bats still inside were old and frail, and he had to nudge some of them awake, and help them toward the exits, explaining hurriedly.

His fur was beaded with sweat when he flew back outside to join Frieda.

"Everyone's out," he panted.

"Good," said Frieda, staring up at the owls. They were still high in the air, but directly overhead now, circling. One owl detached himself from the group, and began a slow descent. He was, Shade noticed, the only one who carried no fire in his claws.

"Go now," Frieda told him, "and take cover in the forest with the others."

"What are you going to do?"

"Talk to the owl."

Shade hesitated. He wanted to stay. He wanted to help. One old bat against these flying giants . . .

"Maybe I should—"

"Go!" Frieda snapped, flaring her wings and baring surprisingly sharp teeth.

Shade went, but not far, only to the nearest tree. He sank his claws into the bark and hung upside down, looking back at Frieda and the huge owl, now settling beside her on Tree Haven's peak.

"Brutus," Frieda said with a respectful nod.

"Frieda Silverwing," came the owl's reply, so deep it was like a roll of thunder.

"You've brought soldiers and fire, Brutus. Why?"

"You know why. We've come for the bat who saw the sun."

Shade felt the owl's words shudder in his bones, and he held his breath, waiting for Frieda's reply. She looked so small beside the owl.

"You cannot make war on us at night, Brutus. That is the law."

Shade was aware of other Silverwings around him in the nearby trees, hanging behind leaves, hunched up on branches, pressing themselves into the bark. Hundreds of dark eyes, fearful and intent, watched Frieda and Brutus.

"The law has already been broken," Brutus said. "We're here for justice. I ask you again, and it will be the last time. Give us the boy."

Shade felt his insides liquify.

"The boy is only a newborn, and he didn't know any better," Frieda said. "Surely you can overlook his foolishness this once."

"The law makes no exceptions."

"Let the owls take him!" It was Bathsheba, flying out from the forest and landing beside Frieda. "Brutus is right. The law has been broken and the boy must pay the price."

Shade could sense the eyes of the other bats on him now, and he burned under their gaze, as if caught in the sun's glare. Did they want him to give himself up? he wondered, a sick gnawing in his stomach. Was that it?

"You know I'm right, Frieda," Bathsheba continued. "One life pays for the law—and protects us all. Where is the boy?"

Shade cast a hopeful net of sound and caught the telltale outline of his mother's upside-down face and shoulders. She turned toward him and their eyes met through a weave of branches of leaves. He'd never felt so alone.

He looked back up at the owls. He knew what they would do if he didn't surrender. All the other bats thought he was a runt, a troublemaker, and now they would think he was a coward. It was his fault: What choice did he have? He closed his eyes, took a deep breath, tensed, and prepared to take flight. Jaws clamped firmly around his rear legs, pulling him back, and he tumbled against Ariel's warm fur.

"Don't you dare," she hissed fiercely.

He hadn't even heard her land.

"They've got fire," he said. "If I don't do it, they'll—"

"They can take me instead."

Shade shook his head in mute horror, and finally realized what danger they were in. The owls wanted a sacrifice, and the thought that it might be his mother . . . it was too terrifying, the idea of losing her. Forever, just like his father. He lunged toward her, digging his claws into her.

"Don't!" he whispered fiercely.

"No!"

It was Frieda's voice from the summit of Tree Haven, and both Shade and his mother turned to look. The elder's wings were spread wide in anger, and she was rising up on her rear claws, teeth bared not at Brutus, but at Bathsheba.

"You forget yourself," she scolded the other bat. "Until I die, I am the chief elder, not you. I am the colony's voice, so hear it now. No one will take the boy, or anyone else." She turned to Brutus. "That is my final reply to you."

The owl's huge eyes hooded. "Your choice is unwise." He beat his wings and lifted from Tree Haven, swiveled his neck and shrieked up to his fellow owls in a language Shade could not understand. Then as Brutus flew higher, he shouted back at Frieda: "You've made your reply; here is ours."

With a terrible shriek, forty owls plunged toward Tree Haven, fire burning in their claws. Shade saw Frieda and Bathsheba fling themselves clear as the owls hurled their sticks at the tree, flames leaping as they struck bark. It can't burn, Shade thought desperately. It's been hit by lightning and it can't burn again. But it did. Sparks caught on the tree's blackened armor, along the branches, up the trunk.

He had to stop it. Before his mother could hold him back, he flung himself into the air and plunged toward a growing patch of flame. He battered it with spread wings, again and again, until it sputtered out. He could do this, he could put out the fires and save Tree Haven. He looked around frantically, and launched himself at another fire. From the corner of his eye he saw his mother and dozens of other bats surge from their hiding places in the forest and soar toward their beloved roost. His heart leaped.

"Put out the flames!" came the cry. "Stop the fire!"

But the owls were waiting for them, and beat them back with their wings as effortlessly as if they were drops of rain. They didn't attack with their claws; their objective was only to keep the bats from the tree. Only a few made it through to fight the flames. Shade finished smothering another small fire, banked around the thick trunk and nearly hit an owl. He veered away just in time. The owl hadn't even noticed him. The giant bird was hovering, pumping his wings, looking for something.

Looking for an entrance.

There was fire in his claws. The owl found the knothole, too small for him to enter, but . . . With a jolt, Shade understood. The owl flew to the knothole and began pushing his fire stick through.

A terrible anger took hold of Shade, filling his head with black. He hurled himself at the burning stick, seizing it in his claws and teeth and trying to wrench it away from the owl. But it was no use. The owl twitched one wing and knocked Shade against the trunk. He was aware of falling in darkness, then a surprisingly gentle thud, and it was only intense heat that brought him around.

He opened his eyes and lurched back from the burning moss at the tree's base. He smacked the fire with singed wings, but it didn't die. The flames grew larger, hungrier, spitting sparks, which caught in his fur and burned his flesh.

"Shade, stop!" It was his mother, pulling him back.

"I've got to!"

"You can't put it out."

Still he struggled, even as she dragged him away through the pall of smoke and up into the air. He knew she was right. Tree Haven was a pillar of fire. And from the knotholes—those entranceways he'd always thought were so secret and safe—shot sharp tongues of flame. Tree Haven was burning inside and out. Bark crackled, ancient wood gasped. There would be no stopping it.

The owls were gone.

His body aching, Shade joined the listless throng of bats in the treetops. He wished he were blind, so he didn't have to see their faces, the looks of shock and anger, or the way the mothers pulled their wings tighter around their children, as if he might somehow hurt them, just by looking at them.

He stared, numb with disbelief and exhaustion, as the flames and thick smoke rose from their doomed home. All his fiery anger seeped out of him and was replaced by a slow, cold fury: This is what the owls did. They killed my father. And now they destroyed my home, our home.

"You're lucky you didn't lose a wing," Ariel said beside him.

He grunted, not caring.

He noticed that the other bats were moving away from them, shuffling to other branches, fluttering silently to other trees. Hadn't they seen him fighting the fire? He'd done his best to stop it!

"Silverwings!" It was Frieda, flying above them. "We must strike out for Stone Hold. If we start now we can make half the distance before dawn and find temporary roosts along the way."

"You have betrayed us, Frieda!" cried Bathsheba, rising into the air and circling angrily. "Look at the ruins of our home. Silverwings, do you still choose Frieda as your leader? The great leader who has let your home burn to the ground! Speak!"

There were ragged mutterings of discontent through

the crowd, though no voice was raised loud enough to stand out.

"My power is only good as long as you give it to me," Frieda told them. "But let me say this. We have suffered a terrible loss tonight. We have lost Tree Haven, our nursery roost for hundreds of years. But no one was killed; we have not lost a single member of our colony. So I say this to you. We can replace our roost, but Ariel could not have replaced her son. All you mothers, who among you would have offered her child in exchange for Tree Haven? Who?"

A miserable silence hung over the assembled bats.

"If I have made the wrong choice, tell me now. But as long as I am chief elder, I will never bargain a life, no matter how terrible the consequences. One life is more important than any roost. You have reason to be angry. Vent your anger at the owls who did this, not one of your own. Speak, anyone who thinks otherwise."

Shade waited in agony as the silence stretched out.

"We have a long journey before us," Frieda said. "To Stone Hold to join with the males—and then on to Hibernaculum."

Slowly, but with grim determination, every bat of the Silverwing colony rose into the air, all the newborns and their mothers, the old and the young. Frieda took the lead with the other elders. She sang as she flew, a high piercing note to blaze their trail.

Shade flew alongside his mother. Never had he known the colony to be so gloomily quiet. He'd spent so much time anticipating the moment they would leave for Hibernaculum. It had both frightened and excited him. But now, he felt deadened, just concentrated on pumping his wings. Flight was a joyless thing to him.

He couldn't stop himself from looking back, until all he could see was the glow of the flames, and the smudge of the smoke's thicker darkness against the night.

By dawn, long after the Silverwings had left, Tree

Haven was still burning. The great branches snapped and exploded, until finally, the tree toppled, heaving its roots up out of the earth and stone, and laying open the cave beneath. And if any bat had been within a thousand wingbeats, he would have heard a million faint voices, streaming up from the echo chamber, their stories released at last, and lost forever in the sky.

They found a deserted barn before sunrise. The rafters sagged, the roof and walls let in dusty shafts of daylight, and the smell of beasts and their droppings was still unpleasantly strong. But it seemed safe, and free of bird's nests. Hanging from the high rotting beams, exhausted, most of the bats plunged immediately into a deep sleep.

Shade pressed close against his mother. His breastbone still ached from the long flight. And whenever he shut his eyes, he saw Tree Haven burning. Ariel shifted and looked at him.

"It's not your fault," she said softly.

"No one's going to talk to me the rest of my life."

"They'll get over it. They saw how brave you were. You tried to save the roost—which is more than most of the others. I'm very proud of you."

Shade glowed silently with her praise.

"Frieda took me to the echo chamber," he told her. It already seemed like such a long time ago.

After a brief pause his mother said, "And what did you hear?"

"The old stories. The Great Battle of the Birds and the Beasts. I heard about the Promise too."

"Not many bats pay attention to those stories nowadays."

"My father did, though, didn't he."

"I suppose Frieda told you." There was annoyance in her voice, and then she gave a small resigned sigh. "She has her reasons, I'm sure. But all I know is that wanting to see the sun gets bats killed. Maybe the stories are true, who knows. Maybe we once flew in the light of day and didn't fear any creature. But now we live in the night, and we've lived in the night for millions of years, and is it really so bad? It's certainly not worth dying for."

"But it's not right," he said doggedly. "We shouldn't be banished. We didn't do anything. And what the owls do—"

"Shade, it's the way things are."

"But what about the Promise? My father thought it had something to do with the bands."

"Well, Cassiel always had unusual ideas. And after he got banded he became more convinced the Promise was about to come true. It was a sign, he thought."

"What was he looking for when he got killed?"

"Wouldn't tell me. He was very excited and said he had to go and check something. But he promised he'd be back in two nights. Maybe he was meeting with other bats. Maybe he was trying to find the Humans who banded him, I don't know. After two nights the whole colony left Hibernaculum on the summer migration. I stayed behind another night, and then one more, just in case. And then I knew the owls must have taken him. So I left and caught up with the others."

Shade didn't say anything. For the first time he could see how terrible it must have been for her. Waiting alone for her mate. Having to give up and rejoin the colony, knowing she would never see him again.

"Frieda said there're others who were banded."

Ariel nodded. "And most of them disappeared too, before Cassiel. There're not many left, a few of the males."

"Maybe they know where he went that night."

She gazed at him fiercely. "It doesn't matter, Shade. Listen to me. I want you to live. When everyone said you would die, and you were too small, I didn't give up. It's a miracle you survived, it really is."

She looked so tired suddenly that Shade pushed his face gently against her fur. He didn't want her to worry. "Sorry," he said.

"Are you scared about the journey south?"

He couldn't remember ever telling her he was, but she seemed to know anyway.

"A little I guess."

"You'll be fine. I'll be with you the whole time. And Frieda makes sure no one ever falls too far behind."

"What if I do, though?"

"Do you want me to tell you about the route we'll take?"

Shade nodded. It seemed like a good idea. Just in case.

"I can't tell you all of it. It would take too long. But I can describe some of the landmarks. Close your eyes and concentrate."

Ariel pressed her forehead against his and began to sing. A brilliant silvery landscape flared up from the darkness: a forest, a clearing, and a high oak rising up, spreading branches. It was Tree Haven.

"You can do it too!" Shade exclaimed, pulling back. "It's just like the echo chamber!"

"I'll teach you how to do it one day. Listen."

She began again, and Shade, eyes clamped tight, watched as his beloved Tree Haven, looking as it did before the owls burned it, became smaller and smaller, fading in the distance, as if he was flying away from it.

Now the magical landscape was changing, dissolving like a thousand pinpricks of light, and suddenly re-forming. He was skimming high over treetops, and then he spotted the barn below, the barn where they were now roosting.

He soared past it, as if he were traveling a million wing-beats a second until, up ahead, he saw a huge Human tower, taller than any tree. What was it? As he hurtled closer, the top of this great tower flashed, and just as quickly blinked out.

He was about to ask his mother what this was, but he was already racing past the tower, and could see that it rose from a rocky clearing on the edge of the water. But this wasn't like the stream where they drank. This black water spread out and out away from the land until it met the night sky in a flat, dreadful line.

"Mom, what is that place?"

"Shade, just listen."

He veered away from the tower, following the bony ridge where the earth met the water, traveling so quickly he felt breathless, as if he really were pounding his wings to keep up.

Then, before him: an upside-down constellation of stars, bigger and denser than the stars themselves, spreading out in all directions.

Then: a metal cross, and the stars swirling around it, and a hollow clanging, *bong, bong, bong,* which made his ears twitch.

And now: one star in the sky, glowing more brightly than the others.

Now: the ears of a giant white wolf, and ice everywhere.

And: a broad torrent of water, crashing, roaring, sending up a spray.

Then his mind went dark with silence. His eyes popped open and he gazed at his mother in wonder.

"Did you see it all?" she asked.

"I think so, but there were things I didn't understand. What was that big tall tower and—"

"I'll explain tomorrow night," she said. "The best thing is just to remember the pictures and sounds I sang to you. They're the most important landmarks on the journey. We should get some sleep. We'll reach Stone Hold tomorrow. You'll get to meet your brothers."

➤ Shade grunted. They'd think he was a runt, probably.

Pressed close against his mother, he wrapped his wings tight around his body, folded his tall ears under for extra warmth. It was colder here than in Tree Haven, and he shivered a few times before warming up. He heard his mother's breathing become soft and slow, and still his mind was busily churning.

There was no point just feeling sorry for what had happened. That wouldn't bring his father back or bring back Tree Haven or stop the owls from hunting them. He would have to do something.

And in the calm floating moments before sleep finally took him, he understood what he must do. At Stone Hold he would meet the other banded bats who knew his father. He would talk to them, get them to tell him what they knew, what really happened to Cassiel. He would find out what the bands meant. Maybe it would mean going to the place where the other bats had disappeared. But he would learn the secret of the Promise. And then he would bring his colony the greatest gift of all.

He would bring them the sun.

# STORM

There was fog as they set out the next night, blanketing the valleys, sifting through the treetops. A sharp wind whistled past Shade's ears and he shivered, his fur beaded with mist.

But he felt strangely invigorated. By dawn he'd be at Stone Hold with the rest of the Silverwings—and the banded males who had known his father. And he had his plan: It was there when he awoke, something fine and solid, like a full stomach. He wouldn't tell his mother, it would just make her worry, and she'd worried enough about him already. Frieda he might tell later, in secret. He knew she would help him.

This morning, before leaving the barn, she'd come to talk to him and his mother. Right in front of everyone. Shade had felt awkward and proud. Here he was, the runty bat Frieda had sacrificed Tree Haven for. He was important, in a way he wasn't entirely comfortable with. Everyone still seemed to be keeping their distance from him. But a few of the newborns said shy hellos to him, before being hurried away by their mothers. From them he got a few curt nods, better than nothing anyway. Maybe they wouldn't hate him forever. Only Bathsheba fixed him with a hard stare as they left the barn, a look that flooded his heart with anger and guilt.

He gazed down now at the strange, ghostly landscape. They were flying above the tree line, and through the splinters of mist, he saw new forests, meadows, streams. Human roads cut through the hills, and one of their noisy vehicles rushed along, shooting out beams of light. A harsh stinging smell rose behind it, and Shade sneezed. He'd seen some of their buildings earlier too, clustered together in clearings, smoke lifting from the roofs.

"Cold?" his mother asked him.

"I'm fine." He wished she'd stop asking. He was determined to prove himself. Even though he was a runt, he'd show the whole colony he wasn't a weakling. He wouldn't ever fall behind and slow everyone down. In fact, he'd do better than that. He'd stay in the front ranks the whole journey, right up there with Frieda and the other elders. He could see Chinook up ahead now, beating his strong wings.

A brisk pungent smell, unlike anything he knew, hit Shade's nostrils. Almost at the same moment, he heard a new sound: It had a deep throbbing rhythm, like some powerful animal, slowly exhaling, breathing in, exhaling again. He looked over at Ariel.

"I'll show you," she said.

She angled her wings and flew higher. Shade followed, and then gasped in wonder. Through the mist he could see the forest end in a ragged line, and give way to mottled darkness, stretching out forever. It was the edge of the world.

Instantly, he remembered his mother's sound map.

"That's all water?" he whispered.

"The ocean."

"There's sure a lot of it."

"It's not like the water in the stream. I took a drink from it once. It tastes salty."

Closer to the land, the water heaved up in huge black and white paws, crashing against the rocks.

"We're not flying over it, are we?"

"No."

Shade was relieved. Just looking at it made him feel very small, and strangely alone. There were no trees, no branches, no rocks or earth. Nothing solid. What if you had to land suddenly? He couldn't swim very well yet, and he certainly didn't want to try down there. He'd heard stories that Humans could float on the water in things called boats. But why would Humans want to do that? What was out there in the sea that could be of any interest to them?

As they flew back down to join the rest of the colony there was a sudden flash up ahead, and Shade immediately thought: lightning. But his mother nodded to a looming shadow on the horizon, hidden behind a band of fog.

"Recognize that?" she said.

The fog cleared, and Shade nodded excitedly. It was the strange high tower from his mother's song, and he was amazed how well she'd described it. As if he'd been here before.

"What's the light?"

"Don't stare at the top," she said. "It flashes every few seconds. It's very bright."

"I remember from your song. But what's it for?"

"Frieda thinks Humans built it long ago to help their boats navigate. And that's how we use it too."

Shade closed his eyes and summoned up Ariel's map. The tower, and then . . . a veering away, following a bony ridge of rock.

"We fly south along the coast, don't we!" he said, understanding. "That's what the map means, right?"

"Good," Ariel said. "We'll always stay over land. It's too dangerous over water. The winds are different."

Frieda led them closer to the huge tower, so that Shade could make out its tapered stone sides, and then the bat elder banked sharply to the south, and the whole colony turned with her, riding the wind above the rocky coast.

The rain started suddenly. Not the gentle drops Shade knew from summer showers, but icy driving needles. They dazzled Shade's echo vision, flaring in his mind's eye like shooting stars. He shook his head, trying to clear it.

"Don't let it throw you off," Ariel told him. "Stick close to me. Feels like a storm coming."

As if on cue, wind tore at his body. He tensed the small bundles of muscle along his wings, trying to keep them taut so he wouldn't get blown off course. Still, the wind buffeted him from side to side, knocking him higher, batting him back down.

"Down to the trees! Down to the trees!" came Frieda's cry, and it was echoed by the other bats. "We'll wait out the storm! Down to the trees!"

The wind screamed around them, and Shade lurched.

"Cling to me, Shade," his mother called out. "It's too rough."

"No!" he snapped. He could still see Chinook up ahead, looking at him over his wing. Shade would not, could not, sink his claws into his mother's fur and cling to her while she flew for both of them. Like he was just a furless pup again. He was special, Frieda had said so. He would land on his own, like Chinook, like the other newborns.

"Shade!" his mother called to him again. "Come here!"

But he intentionally veered away from her, rocking crazily through the rain. He angled his wings to descend.

"I'm fine!" he shouted out.

A savage gust of wind knocked him over onto his back, and his wings buckled.

"Shade!"

"Mom, help!" The wind whipped the words from his mouth. He struggled to right himself, his sodden wings plastered uselessly against his body. Tumbling, he was swallowed up in a bank of fog, unable to see. He had no idea where he was, how high he was off the ground. For a split second the fog opened and he caught a glimpse of his mother and the other bats—so far away, how had they gotten so far away?—and then the fog closed up and he was tumbling again.

At last there was a lull and Shade unfurled his wings. He streamed out from a bank of fog and cried out in dismay.

He was over the ocean.

He wheeled, trying to catch sight of land. But it was lost in the rain and fog. Which way? The stars overhead were blotted out. Another treacherous gust of wind broadsided him, forcing him down. He arched his wings, trying to rise, but he was so exhausted he could barely beat them.

He saw the huge expanse of water below, churning white and black like a million hungry animal tongues. If he hit . . . Again he wrenched his shoulders up, trying to ride higher. But the wind would not let him.

A glimmer of light caught his eye. It twinkled out, came back. Just rain? No, it was coming from something on the water, roughly riding the waves—a boat, it must be a Human's boat. Huge white sails billowed from tall masts.

He trimmed his wings and aimed himself at the boat. The wind shunted him wildly to one side and he soared clear past. Rallying what remained of his strength, he pounded the air and made one last lurching turn back toward the boat. If he missed again he'd be too low for another try.

The boat was dead ahead now, swinging wildly on the horizon. Closer, closer, wings tensed, he neared the tallest mast at breakneck speed, the wind at his tail. He pulled back, braking sharply, claws outstretched.

The sail was thicker than expected, and he almost lost his grip. He sank his claws deeper into the fabric. The sail snapped with the wind, nearly throwing him off.

Inch by inch, Shade crawled toward the mast and into

a tight fold. Sheltered from the wind and rain, he wrapped his wings around his shaking body, and tried to calm the sickness in his stomach. And stop the voice in his head, which kept asking over and over: How are you going to get back? How are you ever going to find them now?

Shade woke with a start.

The boat's violent pitching had given way to a gentle rocking. His whole body ached. Cautiously he pushed his head out from the sail. The sky was still dark, the stars bright, and with huge relief he saw land—a small bay with a few wooden buildings on the rocky slopes.

The boat had brought him back to land!

Maybe his mother and the rest of the colony weren't far away. He flew from the mast, circling, trying to get his bearings. He didn't know if he'd passed this place earlier—they'd flown over a lot of small bays, but they were all veiled in fog, he didn't remember what they looked like.

"Mom?" he cried out hopefully. "Mom?"

His voice echoed back to him from the steep slopes.

He flew inland, eager to get away from the water, and the overpowering briny smell, which he thought must be fish. He soared over the hill, above the tree line, hoping for landmarks. The Humans' tower, maybe he would see that. Nothing but unfamiliar forest stretched out around him.

"Hello?" he called again, with mounting panic.

It was eerily quiet. Maybe if he went lower. He darted down, using his sound sight to steer between silver branches. A squirrel, storing nuts in the crotch of a tree. Silent nests, and sleeping birds, their feet locked around their perches. The whistle of the wind in the dead leaves. In the distance a grunting chorus of toads. But no sign of bats.

He landed on a branch, breathless. Think, he told himself. Think it out. The boat had taken him back to land. But where? Judging from the brightness of the sky, he guessed it was close to dawn. And the storm had hit around midnight. That meant he'd been on the boat for about six hours. How fast did a boat go? He didn't know. What direction was it going? As if he'd had time to notice. Maybe north, maybe south.

He didn't know much about star mapping. Enough to know north and south. He could fly south, and try to catch up with the colony. But what if they'd changed course, gone inland, and he missed them altogether? Or what if the boat had already taken him farther south than the colony? Well, what about north then? Same problem.

This wasn't helping.

Should he just wait here, hoping his mother would come looking for him? But maybe they'd already looked, and just given him up for dead. They'd seen him get blown over the ocean. Well, he could try to find his way back to Tree Haven and—but with a sickening jolt he remembered the burning ruins he'd left behind. Anyway, his mother had told him it was too cold to spend the winter there. He'd freeze to death. *You can't just sit here. Find a way.* He was wasting time.

Wingbeats.

His ears flared. By the rhythm he could tell it wasn't a bird's, and definitely not an owl's. It had to be a bat.

"Hey! Stop!" he cried out, launching himself in the direction of the wingbeats. He threw sound, thought he caught a bright flash of movement, then it disappeared in the foliage. He flew after it, senses straining.

"Come back!" he shouted angrily.

It was gone. He circled for another minute, and then, exhausted, hung from a branch among bright autumn leaves. It was too disappointing. Tears stung his eyes.

"What're you doing here?"

Shade nearly jumped out of his fur. The voice came from the bright curled leaf next to him. He scrabbled away down the branch and peered at it warily, ready to fly. He could see that this talking leaf was much fatter, certainly, than the other leaves, and it actually seemed to be furry in places. He looked for the stem and saw there were actually two, each with a set of five sharp claws.

"You're a bat!" Shade exclaimed.

"You're a genius—of course I'm a bat," came the voice again. The bat shimmered and slowly unwrapped herself. Long wings unfurled, and gave a quick, invigorating shake. Then the wings folded back against bright luxurious fur. Shade could now see her upside-down head. She had a neat pointy nose and elegant shell-shaped ears stuck close to her head. She was young too, though not quite as young as him. Dark eyes met his.

"A Silverwing," she said. "I thought so."

Shade stared. He'd never seen a bat with fur that wasn't the same color as his.

"I'm a Brightwing," she said testily. "Not all bats are the same, you know. I guess you're too little to know that."

Shade bristled, but said nothing.

"I'm Marina."

"Shade."

"So, what *are* you doing here?" she asked again.

"We were heading south down the coast—"

"You and your colony."

"Right, and we got caught in that big storm, and I was blown out to sea."

"You flew all the way out here in that storm?"

"Well, no, I landed on a boat."

"Lucky for you."

"Yeah, it took me back to land." He frowned and looked at her. "What do you mean, 'all the way out here'? Where am I?"

"Well, you're back on land all right, but not where you think. You're on an island."

"A what?"

"An island. You know, a hunk of land with water all around it."

"I'm not back where I started?"

"No."

Shade swallowed. He had to see for himself. He lit from the branch and flew straight up.

Higher and higher he spiraled into the night, and then leveled off, circling. He saw the bay where he'd arrived, and followed the coastline as it curved, around and around and back in on itself, terrifying water stretching to the horizons. All that ocean between him and the rest of his colony. And no sight of land.

"I'll never get back," he whispered.

"It's about a million wingbeats," Marina said cheerfully, swooping up alongside him, and nodding at a point on the horizon. "Not the easiest ride, but definitely not impossible."

"You've done it?"

"Once."

"So you came from the other side too."

She nodded.

He looked at her strangely. "Why?"

"I came here to live. It's not much, I know, but it's home."

He remembered the eerie silence of the forest. Around Tree Haven, there were always hundreds of bats out hunting at night.

"You're all alone here."

"Until you showed up."

"Well . . . where's the rest of your colony?"

"Oh, they're over there somewhere," she said, nodding vaguely at the horizon.

She said nothing more, and Shade didn't see how he could ask. Had she got lost, like him? No, that didn't make sense. She didn't seem upset. But why would you want to live away from your colony? It was unthinkable, that separation. How could you be parted from your parents and brothers and sisters and all the other bats you'd grown up with? Unless she'd been expelled from the colony. He looked at her curiously. What had she done?

"I can point you in the right direction, but it's going to have to be tomorrow night," Marina told him.

He turned to the eastern sky and saw it was beginning to brighten. "Yes," he said. "Thank you."

"You can spend the day in my roost. If you want," she added. "We should probably get going though. No bats on this island, but plenty of owls. Follow me."

# MARINA

She led him under the roof and into the crawl space of an old wooden shack near the bay. The roost she'd made for herself was deep inside a heap of fishing nets, old sails, oily blankets, and muddy leaves, which Shade assumed she'd carried in to stop up any drafts. It was wonderfully warm, and he felt a delicious sense of safety, knowing there were thick soft walls around him. The smell was the only thing—that briny fishy smell.

"You get used to it," Marina told him. "I even kind of like it now."

"How long have you lived here?"

"Since late spring."

"Where will you go for the winter?"

"Thought I'd stay here. Give it a try anyway."

She didn't seem concerned. Shade nodded, wondering if it would be warm enough. He didn't know anything about how cold it would get. It certainly felt warm now. But the idea of her spending the winter here, alone, cold, filled him with sadness, and he thought of his mother, his colony, flying south without him. He rustled his wings impatiently.

"Where were you headed?" Marina asked.

"Stone Hold, to meet with the males."

"Oh, so you're a newborn," she said. "First migration, huh?"

"Yes." He didn't like being reminded of his age. It made him feel small. "How many migrations have you been on?"

"Just two," she said. "One and a half, really."

She shifted on her perch and metal flashed on her forearm.

Shade gasped. How could he have missed it? Then he understood, because she quickly moved again, and he saw that she had a way of always tucking her forearm under her wing so the band didn't show.

"You've got one too!"

She looked at him sharply. "What d'you mean?"

"The band! How'd you get it?"

"You know someone else who has one?"

"Frieda, our chief elder."

Marina's eyes widened. "Your elder has a band, just like mine? You're sure? Like this one here?"

She thrust her forearm toward him.

"Well, I don't know if it's exactly the same, but—"

"How'd she get it?" Marina demanded.

"Humans gave it—"

"How long ago?"

"Well, um, she's pretty old, and she said she got it when she was young, so—"

"Ten, twenty years?"

"At least."

"And she's still alive!" There was awe in her voice.

Shade frowned. "What d'you mean?"

"They said it kills you," she said, but she was smiling.

"Who?"

"The Brightwing elders."

Shade shook his head. "But Frieda never said—"

"Are there any other Silverwings who have bands?"

"A bunch of the males, they got banded last year. Why?"

"And they're still alive too?"

"Some of them," he said tightly. "Others got killed."

"How?" she demanded.

"By owls."

"So maybe my elders were wrong," Marina muttered. "Maybe it doesn't always kill—"

Shade couldn't stand it anymore. "What are you talking about?"

"This!" Marina exclaimed, waving her banded forearm. "This is why I'm here! Alone." She took a deep breath. "Listen. This last spring I was with my colony down south. I'd just finished my first hibernation, and we were traveling back to our summer roosts. Me, my mother and father, everyone."

She paused to catch her breath, and Shade knew she'd waited a long time to tell this story to someone.

"One night I'm hunting along the river, chasing a tiger moth. I'm a long way from the others. And all of a sudden, smack, my wings are all tangled up in some kind of giant web. I didn't even see it with my echo vision. I struggle but can't get free. Then two Humans appear on the riverbank, and start pulling the web in toward them. Their faces are . . . they're blazing with yellow light, like the moon or the sun."

Shade felt his heart purring furiously. Was this what happened to his father? Was this how he'd received his band? Maybe these Humans were the very ones who'd banded Cassiel!

"What happened next?" he breathed.

"One of them plucks me from the net and holds my wings pinned to my sides. Incredible, his strength. I mean, I've never been more scared in my life. I don't know what I'm thinking, that I'll get eaten, I guess, I don't know. So I'm struggling, and twisting, and I try to bite his hand, but my teeth can't get through. He's wearing something over them, tough like animal hide. They keep hold of me, but they're gentle. They stroke my fur, like they're trying to calm me down."

"Did you talk to them?" Shade asked.

"I tried, but it's no good. They didn't understand me. They're talking to each other in these big slow voices like thunder, and I can't figure that out either. So after a while I just give up. One of them holds out my right wing, and the other one, he takes this band of metal and fastens it tight around my forearm.

"So they touch me once more, on the head," Marina said, "and then let me go. I feel—I can't explain it. Like something special has happened to me. So I fly back to the others, all excited. But when my mother sees me, she just stares at the band and starts to cry, and my father just gets this hard look on his face, and there's other bats who take one look at me and fly off scared."

Shade shook his head in confusion. "But why?"

Marina nodded, scratched at her nose. "They thought I was tainted. I mean, I didn't know anything, I'd never heard a thing about these bands. My mom and dad took me to the elders, and I heard it all. It turns out, years ago, a few of the other Brightwings got banded, and they all died or vanished. The stories I heard! One of the bats had his wing rot and fall off, and another bat just caught fire and burned alive."

Shade felt sick, thinking of his father. Was this what happened to him? And the other banded bats who disappeared? Maybe it was the bands that killed them, and not the owls at all.

"But it doesn't make sense," he said aloud, wanting to reassure himself. "Frieda didn't say anything about it, and nothing's happened to her. You're fine too, and you've had the band for months."

"Maybe they were just stories, I don't know," said Marina. "But the elders told me the band was cursed, and that there was nothing I could do. They told me I was . . . what was the word . . . unclean, that's it. I'd been marked by the Humans, and I would only bring bad luck to the colony. So they drove me away."

"No," Shade gasped. "Your mother and father—"

"They couldn't . . . there was nothing they could do," Marina sighed. "They were scared too. I had to say good-bye. At first I tried to follow them from a distance, but the elders sent some big males to chase me away, and eventually I got lost."

Shade could only shake his head in horror. The thought of his own mother, letting him be driven away; it was too painful to bear.

"It was like a bad dream," Marina said. "The first few days I'd kind of forget in my sleep, and I'd wake up and glance around and I was all alone. A few times I ran into other bats, but they took one look at that band and turned tail. By this time I'd hit the coast, and I figured I didn't have long to live anyway.

"I guess I must have been feeling dramatic, because I figured I'd just fly over the ocean and end it all. So I started out and kept saying to myself I'd dive into the water, but it just looked so darn unfriendly. So I thought I'd fly out a little more, and then do it, but I just couldn't quite get the nerve up—all that water, you just knew it was freezing cold—and by then I was so far out there was no turning back. I was downright scared then. Luckily, I caught sight of the island and made it before my wings gave out. And here I am. I mean, it's not so bad. There's plenty to eat, and not a lot of competition."

Shade cast his echo vision over her band, lingering over the strange Human markings. That thin silver ring, closing so perfectly around her forearm. He remembered the beautiful blazing circle of the sun's light, and felt soothed. It was part of the Promise: a sign. It was impossible the band could be anything bad.

"You're so lucky," he murmured, and then winced in regret. It sounded so cruel after all she'd just told him.

Marina snorted. "Yeah, it's done me a world of good."

"No, you don't understand. I mean . . ." He didn't know where to begin. "My father had one, a band." And now his words came tumbling out. He told her about Cassiel, and how he'd disappeared down south; he told her about how he'd seen the sun, and the owls burning down Tree Haven. He told her about the echo chamber, the Great Battle of the Birds and the Beasts, the banishment, and Nocturna's Promise. And he repeated everything Frieda had told him about the bands.

Marina was silent for a long time after he finished. "I tried to rip it off once," she said thoughtfully, "after what the elders said. But it's so tight, like it's always been a part of me. Short of hacking off my claw, that band's here to stay. And you know what? Even when things were at their very worst, there was this little part of me that was glad. I guess I just couldn't believe the band was as bad as they said. There was something . . . important about having it. Something good. I *felt* it."

Shade nodded, envious. Did the Humans choose which bats to band, or was it just luck?

"I knew about Nocturna," Marina said, "and I'd even heard something about the Great Battle—but they never told us anything about this Promise. You really think we can come back into the sun?"

"I don't know how, but I'm going to find out."

Marina looked at him, and grinned. "Quite a little troublemaker, aren't you. Go see the sun, scare your mother half to death, get your roost burned down by the owls. My bet is you're not the most popular bat in your colony right now."

"I guess I'm not," said Shade, and he was grinning too, despite himself.

"I want to meet Frieda and these other bats," Marina said. She wasn't smiling now. "I want to come with you."

# INTO THE CITY

"It can be a rough ride," said Marina the next night. They were heading out over the bay. A crescent moon hung in the clear sky, and there was only a light breeze. "But you shouldn't have too much trouble, even with those stubby wings of yours."

Shade's ears shot up indignantly.

"My wings aren't stubby!"

"Well, they're certainly not as long as mine," Marina said, flaring them briefly. He had to admit, they were longer and narrower—but not by so much. "It's a simple fact. The longer the wings, the faster you fly."

"Mine may be a little shorter," Shade said, "but they're broader too, and that means I'm more flexible in flight." He remembered his mother telling him this when he was learning to fly.

"Hmm," Marina said doubtfully.

"I can even hover. And I can fly through smaller spaces in the forest."

"Interesting. But up here on the high seas, speed's the name of the game, my little friend. And in that department, I've got the edge."

Little friend? She was as bad as Chinook. He hoped he wouldn't regret traveling with her.

"All I know is I made it through that storm last night,"

Shade muttered, "and those winds were pretty bad. I can handle it."

They'd spent an hour feeding around the island, and Shade had gobbled down his food joylessly. All he could think about was how, every second, his mother and the rest of his colony were moving farther away from him. He was desperate to get going, but he knew he had to eat; he'd need all his strength over the water.

As they flew higher, the winds picked up, and Shade felt anxious. Leading the way, Marina's wings billowed impressively with every stroke. Shade grimaced and thought of Chinook.

"How much higher do we have to go?" he asked.

"A bat afraid of heights? That's a new one."

"Just wondering why we have to go so high."

"To find the right slipstream," she explained. "I've played around with them. You sometimes get a current blowing inland, and it'll make the ride a whole lot easier. And faster."

"Oh, right." He didn't like it that she knew more than him.

Angling her wings, she circled for a moment, nose twitching.

"I think we're close. Can you smell it?"

Shade sniffed too, but couldn't detect anything except the pungent odor of the sea. It took all his attention just to keep level in the strong breeze. Wind roared in his ears. He hoped Marina knew what she was doing.

"Just a little more . . . there!"

And Shade felt it too: The wind lulled, and he felt he was being sucked forward. Every wingbeat was like two. He looked down, and regretted it. The ocean, from up here, was nothing more than rippled blackness. He didn't like being so far from trees.

"The mainland's dead ahead. See?" Marina tilted her chin, pointing.

In the distance Shade saw the thin black line of the

coast, and then a tiny but intense flash of light. Darkness again, then another flash.

"That's the tower," Shade said excitedly. "That's where the storm hit."

"The old lighthouse. I remember it. The Humans use it for their boats. It tells them there're rocks ahead, and to steer clear."

She knows everything, Shade thought. She's bigger, even though she's a girl, better at flying, better at everything. And there was her band too.

"So, your colony was headed south, right?"

"For a couple of nights, I think."

"You think?"

"I'm pretty sure."

"We'll catch them along the coast if we're lucky. Depends on how fast they're going. A couple nights maybe. So long as you keep us on route, we'll get there eventually. You know the route, right?"

Shade's stomach felt like he'd just plunged a few hundred feet.

"Well . . ." he said, "my mother sang me a map."

"You've forgotten it?"

"No," he snapped. "I remember everything." He wasn't lying really. He knew he could recall all the sounds and pictures—he just didn't know what they meant. He wished he'd made his mother explain before the storm.

"Well, that's a relief," muttered Marina.

"Anyway, we'll catch them along the coast, right?"

Marina just grunted.

Shade found that the best thing to do was fix his eyes on the flashing lighthouse and will it to draw closer. They talked a little at the outset, then less and less, saving their breath.

The winds held steady, and Shade knew how lucky they were. The eastern sky was beginning to pale as they reached the mainland and banked around the lighthouse. Shade felt exhausted, but exultant. He'd made it back.

Under a toppled birch, they found a secret hollow, and

crawled inside just as the birds' dawn chorus rose from the trees. Instantly he was asleep.

"Wake up."

Shade popped open an eye and stared blearily at Marina. She poked him again with her nose.

"What's wrong?"

"The sun went down half an hour ago."

Night already. He felt like hardly any time had passed. He rustled his wings, and a searing ache spread across the muscles in his chest and back.

"Should've woken me," he groaned.

"Seemed like you needed sleep pretty bad after last night."

"Let's get going."

"Aren't you hungry?"

Of course he was hungry. But it was like torture, knowing there was a long journey ahead, and wasting all that time catching beetles and mosquitoes. Every second was a dozen lost wingbeats.

"They've got to eat too, you know," Marina told him.

He nodded, feeling better. He hadn't thought of that.

"And looks like you could use it. Are all you Silverwings so small?"

"No, they're not," said Shade hotly. "I just happen to be a runt." He almost laughed. Runt. That word was such a big and hated part of his life—he never thought he'd use it in defense. "Anyway, I bet we're better hunters than you Brightwings."

"Think so?" She seemed amused.

"Yeah. Just think about it. We're faster in tight spaces, like around trees where the mosquitoes are. And our fur's darker, so we're better camouflaged. Any insect who's not blind can see you coming a mile away!"

"Well, there's only one way to find out, isn't there?"

"I bet I catch more mosquitoes than you. First one to hit a thousand."

"You're on," she said. "Go!"

They scrambled out from under the fallen birch and darted into the air. While Marina struck out for the tree line, Shade veered through the trees themselves, feeding on dense swarms of mosquitoes, dropping down over small pools of water for newly hatched eggs. He worked out the aches in his body as he flew. Never had he eaten so much, so fast.

He streamed past Marina and they shouted out their scores.

"Six hundred and twenty-five!" he hollered.

"Six eighty-two!"

Know-it-all! He flew faster, twisting and flipping through the air, snapping up every mosquito that flickered across his path.

"A thousand!" he bellowed a minute later. "I did it! Where are you?"

"What took you so long?" said Marina, hanging from a nearby branch, leisurely grooming her wings.

"You got a thousand?"

"Hm-hmm."

"You didn't!"

"A few seconds ago, actually."

"Well, you didn't say anything," grumbled Shade, landing beside her.

"You didn't hear me." She burped loudly.

"You know, I don't feel so good," he said.

"Serves you right."

"Me? What about you? It was your idea!"

"Look, I don't feel too jaunty either," Marina admitted.

"I never want to eat another mosquito in my life."

"Did they seem unusually spicy to you?" she asked.

"Please, don't talk about it."

It took a while before their stomachs settled enough for them to fly. Shade felt like he'd swallowed a large stone.

"Let's call it a tie," said Marina after a while.

Shade smiled and gave a deafening burp. "Sounds fair to me."

They kept up a good pace through the night.

It was the coldest yet, the grass sparkling with frost. They kept the coastline on their left wingtip. There was a Human road snaking along the shore as well, and by now Shade was used to seeing their vehicles race along it.

"Do you think the Humans will help us somehow?" Marina asked.

"That's what my father thought."

"I've been thinking about the Promise. About coming back into the light. Wouldn't we go blind?"

"Only if you stared right at the sun for a long time," Shade said. In the cold night he remembered its heat, its sheer power.

"But you just saw a bit of it, right?"

"Well, yeah, but Frieda saw all of it. They just don't want us to have it, the other birds and beasts. Know what I think? If we could get the sun, we'd grow, and we wouldn't have to worry about the owls hunting us. We can ask the other Silverwings—the males who are banded." He stared at the horizon. "If we ever catch up."

"You said they'd follow the coast for a while. Then what? How do we know when to change course?"

"I could try singing you the next bit maybe." Not that he'd been taught, but he thought it was worth a try. He was good at catching echoes . . .

"It won't work."

"It won't?"

"Don't you know anything? You're a Silverwing, I'm a Brightwing. Our echoes aren't the same. It'd just be a big mess."

"So only I can read the map," he said, and couldn't stop a grin. He liked that. Something he knew that she didn't.

"Don't look so cocky about it. You'll have to explain it to me best you can."

He called up his mother's sound map. He saw the ocean, the lighthouse, the coastline, and then—

"Lights," he told Marina. "Like stars, only they're not really. And they're down on the ground instead of in the sky. And it's like everything's made of the light. Giant shapes . . ."

"A city," Marina said simply.

Shade blinked. That was easy. "You've been there?"

"Once. We've really got to go in there?"

There was something important in that city, in the midst of all that light. A tower, higher than the lighthouse . . .

"Yes. There's a landmark. We use it to set course, something to do with the stars and a metal cross . . ."

"Listen!" Marina said suddenly, cutting him off.

Shade's ears twitched, strained, and he could hear the unmistakable creaky flutter of wingbeats. Not just one set, but many.

"Come on!" With a burst of speed he soared through the sky until, in the distance, he could see the bats with his echo vision, hundreds of them shimmering out across the tree line.

"I think it's them!" he told her. "It must be!"

"I hope they like me," said Marina. "How should I introduce myself? Hi, I'm a friend of the bat who got your roost burned down."

Shade laughed aloud with delight. "Hey! Hello!" he called out at the colony. "It's me, Shade!"

Three bats toward the rear banked and looked back. Shade swept over them eagerly with his echo vision. Yes, the wings were the right shape, the tails, the bodies a little large maybe, but . . .

"No," he breathed in disappointment as he drew closer. They were Graywings, luxuriously furred, with handsome sideburns on their faces. Even their ears were rimmed with gray fur, and the underside of their forearms too.

"Where are you two headed?" one of them asked.

"We're looking for the Silverwing colony," Shade said. "Have you seen them?"

"We came in from the northwest. We saw a few other colonies, but not Silverwings. Which way were they headed?"

"South down the coast, toward a city."

"Probably not far ahead of us, then. You get lost?"

"Two nights ago, in a storm."

"Bad luck. Well, I don't envy you, going into the city. It's not a good place for bats. Look, we're going around the city, but we'll continue south after that. You're free to come with us for a while, if you like."

He saw them all up ahead, mothers and fathers flying with their children, veering off quickly to catch food as they went. He glanced at Marina. It was tempting. Flying with a big group. Maybe it wasn't so important to go into the city. Maybe they could stay on course without finding the tower.

All at once the Graywing veered away from them, staring at Marina's forearm.

"She's banded," he hissed to Shade.

"I know," he said.

"Are you out of your mind?" the Graywing said, circling from a distance. "It's bad luck, very bad luck. She's been touched by Humans. Didn't your mother teach you anything? She'll bring doom on all our heads."

"No," Shade said, "it's not—"

"You're welcome to travel with us, Silverwing—but not her."

Shade stared at the Graywing, at the colony of bats in the distance.

"If she can't come, I'm not coming either."

"Suit yourself. But I'd watch out for her if I were you."

The Graywings darted back to their colony, and then, on cue from their elder, swung inland, away from the water, away from them. Shade felt heavy with disappointment. His thoughts had leaped ahead of him, imagining his mother.

"Sorry," said Marina. "I forgot to cover the band. I thought they were yours."

"It doesn't matter," he said. "I just don't understand. Why do they think the bands are bad luck?" He looked at the silver ring around her forearm, and for the first time, felt a prick of uneasiness. "Something must have happened, more than just stories."

"Maybe you should've gone with them," she said tersely.

"That's not what I mean."

"Nothing's stopping you."

"I'm not leaving—"

"You think I need your company? I'm used to living alone. I don't need you or your colony, Shade." She stared at him, her eyes hard, then looked away. "I'm . . . forget it."

"Maybe there're different kinds of bands," Shade said. "Good ones and bad ones." His head ached, and his stomach felt queasy. "I don't know."

"And which have I got? Guess I'll know when I burst into flames."

Shade stared at her in alarm, and they both laughed, long and hard, until he felt the tears come to his eyes. But he still couldn't shrug off his anxiety. If only they could reach his colony, and get some answers.

"Sorry they weren't your colony," Marina said.

"Yeah."

"We'll catch up. That map of yours is doing the job."

Shade smiled gratefully. Ahead of them he could see a ghostly brightening on the horizon, as if the sun were about to rise. Only he knew this wasn't the sun.

"Here comes the city," said Marina.

# PART TWO

# GOTH

Tonight he would be free.

Goth hung from a sinewy branch in the artificial jungle. It was hot here, but the heat didn't come from the blazing tropical sun; it came from some hidden underground furnace. The drizzling rain and mist didn't come from the sky, but from tiny sprinklers in the flat black ceiling. Goth could tell that even some of the plants were fake, their fronds stiff and odorless. Did the Humans really think he was so stupid?

This place was nothing like his home, the real jungle, where they'd captured him a month ago. This place was a prison—he could circle it in a few hundred beats of his powerful wings. When they'd first put him inside, he'd smashed into the invisible walls, foolishly trusting his eyes when he should have relied on his echo vision. These walls were strong as stone; but by some magic Goth didn't understand, his eyes could see right through them, to the place where the Humans came and went, peering in at him.

Didn't they realize who he was? A prince of the royal family, Vampyrum Spectrum, and a descendant of Cama Zotz, the bat god, and ruler of the Underworld. All men and women were sent there when their bodies died. They came face-to-face with Zotz himself, and he would decide their fate, ripping off the heads of those who had displeased him during their earthly lives.

In Goth's home, Humans worshipped Zotz. Women about to have babies would come to the royal cave and pray, asking that their children be strong and healthy and live long. They left offerings—food and flowers, and sparkling disks of metal.

But the Humans here . . . He glared at the band they'd fastened around his forearm. The mark of a prisoner. It was an outrage. When he escaped he would return to the royal cave and call upon Cama Zotz to punish them.

Especially the Man.

He wore white robes, and was tall, with spindly arms and legs. He had wiry black hair and an unkempt beard. One of his eyes was always half closed, giving his face, at first glance, a sleepy look. But the eyes themselves were anything but sleepy, bright and hard. Sometimes the Man flashed searing lights in his face; sometimes he came into the artificial jungle and stuck a dart into his side that made him plunge into a deep sleep. Mostly he just sat on the other side of the invisible wall and stared.

Restless, Goth tensed the powerful muscles of his massive chest and unfurled his wings to their full three-foot span. He had a large angular head crested with bristly fur. He had tall pointed ears, and a strange flat nose, which flared upward into a spike. His eyes were large, unblinking, and pitch black. A long snout, more like that of a beast than a bat, housed a set of glistening teeth. His entire body was taut, as if ready at any moment to slash down and attack.

The Humans fed him mice, tiny, cowering things. He was tired of the taste: meek and watery, as if they'd all come from the same brood. He craved variety.

Above all he craved bat, live, pungent bat flesh.

He longed to hunt again.

There was another prisoner here, a bat called Throbb. They'd been caught together, hunting in the same part of the jungle. Goth had never liked Throbb; he was not of royal blood—a weak, lying creature who fed on the rotting carcasses left behind by other animals. He probably hadn't even struggled as the Humans took him.

Goth had quickly marked out his own territory, relegating Throbb to a small corner. Occasionally he fought Throbb for his mice, not because he was hungry, but because it was something to do, and it amused him to see Throbb back away, whimpering. From time to time he'd even thought of eating Throbb—that's how desperate he was for bat meat. But even though he detested the other bat, he needed him. To help him escape.

And tonight he would be free.

From his roost he watched as the Man approached the invisible wall and opened a secret door. Goth had been watching him do this, night after night. At first he'd thought maybe this was his way out. When he was sure he was alone, he'd found the whisker-thin outlines of this secret door, and many times had tried to open it himself, battering it with his head, trying to sink his claws into the hard, slippery surface. But it was hopeless.

Then, one night, he'd noticed a current of cool air moving through the jungle. Circling, he'd found the source. In the black ceiling was a small metal grate, through which he could feel a draft. He'd tried desperately to squeeze his body through one of the slits, but he was too large, even with his wings folded tight against his sides. He'd have to move the whole grate. And it would be much faster with help.

"Do you want to get out of here?" he'd asked the other bat.

"Of course," replied Throbb warily. "But how?"

"Work with me, and you'll soon be free in the jungle."

So, night after night, when the Humans had left, the two bats flew up to the grate and, with their claws and teeth, chipped away bits of cement and plaster around the edges. Every night the grate was a little looser.

Now, he watched as the Man tipped a dozen white mice onto the ground. He shut the door and sat down behind the invisible wall, watching. Goth stared back at him, hating him. Why didn't he go away? Did he have to watch everything?

Throbb was already pouncing down on the mice, trying desperately to eat as many as he could before Goth showed up. Goth had no appetite, but knew he would need all his strength tonight. He fed quickly, sometimes breaking their necks with a quick chop of his jaws, sometimes swallowing them whole, so he could feel them wriggling down his throat.

"Go back to your roost and pretend to sleep," he hissed at Throbb.

Hanging upside down, one eye open just a slit, Goth waited in agony. He tried to think of his coming freedom. He would fly back into the jungle and rejoin his family. He'd become a great hero, escaped from the Humans' prison!

Finally the Man stood and walked away, and darkness fell behind the invisible wall. Goth lit from his roost.

"Now!"

Together, they flew to the ceiling, locking claws around the metal grate. They strained with all their might to drag it loose, but still it held fast.

"Put your wings into it!" growled Goth.

They unfurled their wings, and began beating them furiously, driving back from the ceiling. Dust showered Goth's fur.

"Harder!" he roared at Throbb. "Harder if you want your freedom!"

They heaved again and Goth felt the grate give way in a cascade of rubble. It was heavier than he'd bargained for, and his wings buckled. He plunged backward with Throbb, the grate riding on top of them. Throbb twisted out from underneath and swooped clear, but Goth's claws were still caught around the metal slits.

"Zotz!" he roared. And suddenly his claws ripped free and he flipped over onto his side and away. The grate pounded into the damp earth.

Goth clung to a vine, waiting for his heart to slow. Zotz had come to his rescue.

"Are you all right?" he heard Throbb call out.

"No thanks to you."

But he was in too much of a hurry to waste time beating Throbb. He flew to the hole, clung to the edge, and poked his head up. A cool breeze played on his slick fur. He sang out and let the returning echo draw a picture in his head.

It was a metal shaft, leading straight up. It was too narrow for them to even spread their wings. Walls too smooth for their claws.

"We'll have to fly straight up."

Throbb whimpered doubtfully.

"Stay behind if you want," Goth said, folding his wingtips in. The strain on his bones was tremendous as he pounded the air furiously, wings a blur, fifteen, twenty, twenty-five beats a second, his heart beating just as fast.

And he was rising up into the shaft, rising like a dark angel from the Underworld, up and up, jaws grinding in exertion, saliva bubbling at the corners of his mouth. He heard nothing but the volcanic roar of his heart. Just when he thought his wings would snap, the shaft suddenly opened into a horizontal tunnel. He dropped gasping to the flat metal surface.

No time to rest. Turning his face into the wind, he began to crawl quickly along the floor, not even waiting for Throbb to catch up. The breeze was stronger here, and he strained to catch the familiar scents of the jungle, but couldn't. Never mind—he was almost there.

There was a sound, a fast, deliberate chopping, getting louder.

*Chomp-chomp-chomp-CHOMP-CHOMP*

He rounded a corner and was blasted by air, making

him squint. At the end of the tunnel, beyond a mesh screen, was a huge twisted blade, spinning.

"What is that?" Throbb asked, hurrying after him.

"Do you think I know everything about Humans? It's some kind of trap to keep us inside."

"It'll cut us to pieces!"

Goth ignored him. Beyond that blade was the night. He could smell it. Zotz would not let him be defeated. He focused all his attention on the revolving blade, listening carefully. The metal mesh was not finely woven; they could get past that with their wings closed. But the blade . . .

It spun in a circle at the end of the square tunnel, leaving a small crescent of free space in each of the four corners. Goth quickly measured the distance in his mind.

"Squeeze through," he told Throbb.

"What?"

"In the lower corner, you can squeeze through. The blade won't hit you."

He wasn't absolutely sure of this, which was why he wanted Throbb to go first.

"Maybe there's another way out," said Throbb. "The other tunnel . . ."

Goth shoved his bared teeth close to Throbb's face.

"You'll do what I say," he hissed.

Slowly Throbb slunk down the tunnel. Wings squeezed tight against his shaking body, he neared the mesh screen. He pushed halfway through, and came to a sudden stop, staring at the whirling blade as if hypnotized.

*Chomp-chomp-chomp—*

"It's too fast," he called back over his shoulder. "It's going to suck me in."

*Chomp-chomp-chomp—*

"Do it!"

"I can't."

Goth darted forward and bit Throbb's tail. With a yelp, the other bat lunged forward. Goth listened as the huge blade cut swiftly through the air. Throbb cried out in terror as the tip sang past him, slicing a patch of fur from his shoulder. But he was through.

Goth's heart leaped. He hurried forward, squeezed through the mesh, and let out all his breath. The blade was so fast it created a whirlwind effect. He stiffened against its pull, listening to the blade in his mind's eye.

He sprang forward.

*Chomp—*

The blade's passage was like a thunderclap, blinding him in one ear.

But he'd made it through unharmed.

And he was suddenly outside.

He unlocked his wings and lifted into the night air.

"Free!" he roared in triumph, but his cry caught in his throat.

Where was the jungle?

A galaxy of bright lights spread out dizzyingly before him, steep canyons and deep glowing rivers of sound. Huge stacks of stone and light towered all around him. Goth wheeled in tight circles, not knowing where he was. He'd expected the jungle to greet him, the familiar sights and smells of dense rain forest, the cry of his bat brothers and sisters.

But this landscape was utterly alien to him. The noise from below was almost overwhelming, making his vision blur and pulse. He could make out only a haze of movement.

He shivered violently, and only then did he notice how bitterly cold it was. The jungle was never this cold. His hatred of the Humans doubled. Where had they taken him? In panic he gazed up at the stars.

He did not recognize a single one.

They were all different.

And where was the moon? He spiraled higher, hoping he would see the jungle just on the horizon. But the lights spread on endlessly. He could not even see the glow of the sun. That would at least have given him a sense of direction.

Maybe, he thought in panic, there was no sun here, no west or east, north or south.

"Where are we?" wailed Throbb, flapping alongside him.

But all at once the moon appeared from behind a bank of clouds, and Goth's heart surged with relief. This was something he recognized, with all its familiar bumps and creases.

"The Humans must have taken us out of the jungle," he told Throbb. "They've taken us north." He'd heard stories, terrible stories.

"It's so cold. Let's go back inside," said Throbb.

"What?" hissed Goth in disgust. "To our prison?"

"It's warm at least."

"No, I'm going back to the jungle."

"But who knows how far that is?"

Goth looked at Throbb contemptuously. Originally, he'd planned to eat Throbb after they'd escaped. A little victory celebration. But now, in these strange surroundings, he didn't think it wise to kill Throbb just yet. He was in a foreign land, and he was not at all sure of himself. He might need help again.

"We'll find a way back," he said through clenched teeth. "And we'll get there, one wingbeat at a time."

"We'll freeze."

"Shut up!" snapped Goth.

He was cold and he needed more food. Food to keep him warm.

He cast his powerful sonic eye over the peaks of the city. The echo brought him back an image of birds roosting on the ledge of a high square tower.

Pigeons. Plenty of meat on them.

He flexed his claws and plunged.

# PIGEON

Shade and Marina flew over the city, dazzled. An endless latticework of light streamed hypnotically to all horizons. Machine sounds seeped up from below—metallic honks and grindings, and a pervasive throb, which seemed part of the air itself. For a dizzying moment Shade could almost imagine the Humans' lights really were stars, and he was flying upside down.

He was exhausted. They hadn't eaten much since entering the city. There were fewer insects here, and those he'd caught had a nasty taste, sooty and unfamiliar. All he wanted was to find the landmark, get his bearings, and get out.

They were crossing a black harbor now, and ahead of them on the opposite shore was a square stone tower, thrusting hundreds of feet into the sky. It wasn't like the lighthouse. This tower was much more ornamented, with ledges and carvings, and numerous windows, some bright, some dark. On one side, near the top, was a massive white circle, bigger than the moon, and brighter. Black markings were inscribed around the inside rim, and Shade could hear a regular clicking from behind the flat circular face. Capping the tower was a steep turret, rows of gabled windows set into the sides.

"Is this it?" Marina asked impatiently.

Shade conjured up his mother's sound map and tried to make a match. A tower, a high-peaked turret—it seemed to fit . . .

From inside came a huge resonant bonging sound, making Shade and Marina both flinch. *BONG!* Then another. *BONG!* And another. *BONG!* Then silence.

"The sound from the map," said Shade excitedly. "This must be the right place!"

They swung in toward the turret, and landed on some wooden slats nailed haphazardly across a gabled window. Hanging upside down, Shade frowned up at the turret, studying its sharp silhouette against the night sky.

"No," he said, "there's something missing." And then it came to him. "The metal cross. There's no cross on this tower. We've got the wrong one."

"Shade . . ." said Marina softly. "Do you smell that?"

For the first time he noticed the thick unpleasant odor wafting out from the window. With a flash of plumage, a huge head thrust out from between the broken slats and closed its beak around his forearm. He stared in horror at the flashing eye, too shocked to feel any pain. The next thing he knew he was torn from his roost, and pulled through the window and into the turret.

Battered by wings, he was dragged roughly through the air. He saw and heard only glimpses of things: windows, wooden planks, the bodies of more birds, a kind he'd never seen before—all spinning as he was hauled down and down, his forearm pincered in the bird's beak.

"We've got two of them!" a bird's voice shouted. "Awake! Awake!"

Finally he was slammed against the floor and released, and then Marina came crashing down beside him with a groan. They were in some kind of pit, covered with sticky bird droppings. The stench was so overpowering he almost retched. The two birds who'd caught them now dragged a tar shingle over the opening, trapping them.

"Wake the captain!" came another voice from above.

"Pigeons," Marina breathed.

"You've seen them before?"

She nodded. "They run the city skies. They're everywhere."

"But . . . why weren't they asleep?"

She was shaking her head. "It's like they were waiting for us . . ."

"They can't do this. We weren't doing anything. The night's ours."

"Somehow, I don't think they care. We've hit a patrol roost. Lucky us."

The pit wasn't very big. Between the wooden planks underfoot ran whiskers of light, and Shade could hear a rhythmic ticking from below. He knew the light must be coming from that strange bright circle on the tower.

He fluttered up to the shingle, and pushed gently. It didn't budge. The pigeons were standing right on top of it, and he could see the points of their claws, pressing through. They'd never get out that way.

"What do they want with us?" he whispered, dropping back beside Marina.

Suddenly the shingle was jerked back and the heads of two pigeon guards plunged down and grabbed them. They were hauled from the pit and dropped onto the floor. He huddled close to Marina, hurriedly taking in the surroundings.

They were at the bottom of the turret. Wooden beams crisscrossed overhead like a giant web. And roosting on the beams were dozens and dozens of birds, growling indignantly, angrily cracking their wings.

"More light!" roared one of the guards.

Across the floor Shade saw two pigeons dragging at another tar shingle, and suddenly a shaft of blinding light surged up into the turret. He narrowed his eyes to slits, listening to the terrifying flurry of activity, listening for ways out.

Even if they could get airborne fast enough, they'd

have to weave their way through all those beams. And get past all the birds. Shade could hear pigeons barring the windows, wings flared, beaks snapping. They weren't as big as owls, but they were still many times larger than him, with huge chests and muscular wings—and those eyes, those weirdly sparkling eyes.

Overhead, every beam was lined with birds now, peering down at them malevolently. The whole turret throbbed with the sound of their low ominous growling—*coorrrr, coorrrr, coorrrr*—making Shade's ears twitch.

Then, on one low beam, the line of birds parted respectfully as a big pigeon strutted forward, chest thrown out, head held high. An angry raised scar ran from his face down the length of his throat.

"Make your report, Sergeant."

"Yes, Captain, sir!" said the pigeon next to Shade with a smart jerk of his head. "We caught these two bats just outside the turret!"

"Good work, Sergeant." The captain glowered down at Shade and Marina. "Are these the two you saw, Private?"

Another lean soldier pigeon fluttered down to the beam and peered at them. There was a gash in his right shoulder, which was still oozing, and he seemed extremely nervous, his head flicking from side to side. His eyes burned.

"No," he said instantly, and then started laughing frantically. "These two? No. No, no, no. They're too small. The ones I saw were . . ." The pigeon twitched violently, and he stopped laughing. Fear poured from his haunted eyes. "Huge, Captain, sir. They were huge, their wings spanned at least three feet . . ."

"Enough," snapped the captain angrily, and after a few startled grunts, the other pigeon fell silent, his head ticking back and forth.

Shade felt sick. He looked helplessly at Marina. What were they talking about? Bats with three-foot wingspans . . .

"Where are the other bats?" the captain shouted down at them.

Shade didn't know how to reply. Which bats? Was he talking about Silverwings?

"I don't know what you mean—"

The pigeon guard pecked him sharply with his beak, and Shade cried out.

"What were you doing around our roost?"

"We're migrating," Marina said. "We're trying to find a landmark to help us on our way south. We thought this was the right tower but—"

"Who killed my two guards earlier tonight?"

Bats killing pigeons? Shade swallowed. They couldn't . . . but three-foot wingspans? It was a mistake. No bat was that big.

"We don't know."

"Where are they roosting?"

"We don't—"

"How many are there?"

Shade looked at Marina. He knew it was pointless to talk now; they weren't listening, and he felt afraid. Afraid of their sparkling beaks, the anger that seemed to be welling up inside the turret like a thunderhead.

A pigeon guard fluttered down to the captain.

"Sir, the ambassador has arrived."

"Excellent." He turned back to Shade and Marina. "I think you'll find the ambassador is less patient than me."

High in the turret, a dark shape loomed in one of the windows, and Shade saw the outline of a she-owl. Behind her, two other guard owls circled outside.

"Things just got much worse," he muttered to Marina.

He watched as the owl ambassador entered the pigeon roost slowly, almost disdainfully, her head swiveling slowly from side to side. Her nose twitched. A hush fell over the roost, and the captain flew up to greet her.

"Ambassador, welcome. Thank you for coming on such short—"

"You've caught the killers?" came the low terrifying voice.

"No, Ambassador, they're too small, but—"

"Where are they?"

The owl dropped to a perch close to the floor. Her flat eyes took in Shade and Marina. Shade trembled.

"They're spies," growled the she-owl.

"No!" Shade protested.

"They deny it!" cried the captain angrily, and the other birds cracked their wings in outrage, their growls deepening.

"Then why were you caught directly outside the pigeons' roost?" the ambassador asked.

"We were lost!"

"You know nothing of the bats who killed the two pigeons?"

"No," Shade insisted.

"They were probably gathering information for another attack," the owl told the captain. "I suggest you ready your soldiers."

"Yes, Ambassador."

"Have they told you the location of the others?"

"No."

"I see."

The owl turned her gaze back on Shade.

"Silverwing," said the owl thoughtfully. "Where are you from?"

Shade said nothing.

"Answer!" shouted the captain.

"The northern forests."

"Yes, I thought so. One of their bats broke the law and looked at the sun."

Muttered outrage swept through the turret.

"We burned their roost to the ground several nights ago. I suspect the same bats are responsible for this latest atrocity, Captain. Some pathetic act of revenge, perhaps."

"We will crush them!" said the captain.

"Not if there's more like the others I saw," muttered the soldier pigeon with the gash in his shoulder. And he laughed, a quick strangled laugh.

"That's enough, Private!" snapped the captain.

"I'm not going back out there to fight 'em, Captain . . . I'm not . . . they've got claws, sir, and teeth like—"

"Silence!"

"It's the gargoyles, that's what they is, them gargoyles on the cathedral come to life . . . I know it . . ."

"Guards, take him away!" The captain turned apologetically to the owl. "Private Saunders has a tendency to exaggerate."

"No bat can be a match for birds," said the owl calmly. "I bring an order from the king of the Northern Realms," the owl announced. "Hear the king through me. The skies are now closed. This murder of birds by bats is an act of war, and we will respond in kind. The law is broken."

The owl turned her baleful eyes on Shade.

"You bats are no longer protected in the night. Any bat seen in the sky, night or day, is subject to death. We will not tolerate these actions. Our messengers have already been dispatched to all nests in the city, and will travel beyond as fast as our wingbeats."

"You can't do this!" Shade shouted in fury.

The nights, closed. That meant none of them were safe now. He thought of his mother and the rest of his colony. Were they far enough away, or would the owls' decree catch up with them? More than ever, he knew he had to reach them.

"It has already been done, little bat," said the owl. "And if you value your life, you will tell us where we can find the killers."

"We don't know anything."

The owl turned to the captain. "I must go make my report to the royal assembly. Torture these two until they talk, then send for me."

"Yes, Ambassador."

The owl flared her wings, and the pigeons cleared a path for her as she rose regally through the turret and disappeared into the night sky.

"Prepare the bats for amputation," the captain told his guards.

Shade felt all his joints turn loose and watery.

"What does that mean?" he asked Marina. "Amputation?"

"I don't know," she stammered, "I don't—"

"Peck!" came the low ominous chant from the birds. "Peck, peck, peck, peck."

*Scriiiiiiittttttcchhhhhh!*

Shade's ears twitched in terror. A group of pigeons were dragging their beaks against the stone.

*Scriiiiiiittttttcchhhhhh! Scriiiiiiittttttcchhhhhh!*

Shade suddenly understood. They were sharpening their beaks.

"Your punishment will be the loss of your wings!" decreed the captain. "You can crawl back to your bat friends and tell them that the pigeons of this city will not forget this outrage. Take hold of them!"

"Take their wings!" cried the guard on the ground. "Pin them down!"

Pigeons dropped from their perches and began to crowd in. They were going to take away his wings, peck them off so he could never fly, never reach home. He felt powerless and naked in the bright light. The light.

"Follow me!" he hissed to Marina.

He sprang forward, leaping over the ring of pigeons and landing on the floor beyond them, very near the blinding shaft of light. He shut his eyes. Flaring his wings, he tripled his size in an instant, and bared his teeth with a bloodcurdling shriek. Three pigeons scattered in astonishment. Marina landed beside him. Shade felt for the rough surface of the tar shingle.

"Push!" he urged her. "Block the light!"

Together they sank their claws in and pushed. The shingle slid quickly across the floor.

"Take hold of them!" roared the captain. "Seize their wings!"

But the turret was plunged into total darkness. Shade knew now was their only chance. The pigeons were momentarily blind.

"Come on," he hissed to Marina.

Slowly he lifted off the ground, drumming his wings frantically. With his sound vision he scanned the turret: the silver webwork of beams, pigeons fluttering blind in panic, their wings etching ghostly shadows in his mind's eye. He spotted the nearest window: a beckoning rectangle of blackness. He plotted his course.

The pigeons fluttered in confusion, smacking into one another. Shade veered around one beam, then another, his wings jerking sharply from side to side. From behind, a pigeon knocked him in the side of the head, stunning him. He dropped to a wooden beam.

"Got one!" the pigeon cried.

"Shade!" he heard Marina cry beside him.

"Go!" he shouted. "I'm okay."

But he felt the bird's heavy wing press down on him hard, trying to pin him. Instinctively he sank his teeth into the feathers and hit flesh. The pigeon yelped and the wing snapped up.

Shade leaped from the beam, dropping several feet before his wings could lift him again. Where was Marina? He cast a panicked sonic glance around and saw her slender outline, making for the window above him. She flashed through and was out. A pigeon lunged to block his path, but Shade flipped sideways just in time, and soared through the window, back into the night.

# KEEPER OF THE SPIRE

Six pigeons burst after them from the turret windows.

Shade shot a look over his wing, saw the birds fanning out across the sky to hem them in.

"Can we outrun them?" he gasped.

"Don't think so," panted Marina.

"They've got to be half blind out here!"

"Plenty of light."

She was right. It wasn't like night in the forest. Light poured up from the city. They streamed over it, swinging wildly around towers, skimming rooftops, plunging down into deep canyons. His fear was shot through with exultation: He was back in the night, his own element. No bird could catch him. He was small, black as the sky, quick as a shooting star. Still the pigeons kept doggedly after them.

"Follow me," Marina said.

He spun down into the city after her. Past walls of light, moaning machinery, Human vehicles on the glittering roads.

"Where are we going?"

"Somewhere dark."

She dropped down into a narrow alley between two low buildings, and he plunged after her, piercing the deep shadows with his echo vision.

"Here!" she called out.

They rounded a corner and threw themselves against a sooty brick wall, clinging with their claws. For good measure, Shade spread his black wings over Marina's body, making them all but invisible in the darkness. They stopped breathing as the pigeons thrashed past over the alley, then circled.

"Where'd they go?" said one soldier.

"That way, I think."

"Go. We'll check here."

Two soldiers stayed behind and settled on the rooftop's edge, listening, their heads ticking from side to side. Shade watched them with his echo vision.

"It's too dark," said the first soldier. "I can't see a thing."

"We've lost them," said the second.

"Let's head back."

"The captain won't be happy."

"But what if those big ones come back . . ."

"Forget what Saunders said. He's a liar. There're no bats like that."

"Then how'd they kill two of us? You saw that wound on Saunders's shoulder."

"Maybe they had weapons, how do I know?"

"He said they carried the bodies away in their claws."

The other pigeon had no reply to this.

"All right. Let's go back. Call the others. It'll be light in a few hours. We can send another team at dawn."

They lit from the rooftop and disappeared. When he could no longer hear them, Shade hungrily sucked in air. He felt like he hadn't taken a breath in hours.

Marina pushed away his wings. "Nearly suffocated me under there," she said indignantly.

"Yeah, well it worked," he shot back with a grin. He was so glad to be free of the turret. Glad both his wings were still attached to his body.

"You can thank me for that," she said. "They'd have caught us in the open."

"Hey, I was the one who killed the light and got us out of that stinking turret!"

"That was quick thinking," she admitted.

"Sure was."

"And a lot of luck," she added. "We're lucky to be alive."

Shade shrugged. His whole body was buzzing. "They weren't so tough. They're not great fliers, are they? I mean, they're not as fast as us, and they're noisy for one thing, and they can't maneuver very well. What an escape!"

"They'll come back for us."

He sighed. She was so sensible. It started to rain gently, and he felt suddenly very tired.

"We've got to find the right tower," he said. But how would they ever find the right tower in this city of towers? All he wanted was to be out of the city, and on their way again.

"Let's find a safe day roost first. I don't want to be caught out by dawn, with every bird in the city hunting us."

Closed skies. The owl's words echoed in Shade's head. They'd never be safe now. All his life the night had been his, now it was taken away. And all because the pigeons said bats had killed two of them. Giant bats.

"What are gargoyles?" he asked Marina.

"I don't know. You thinking of what that pigeon said?"

"Maybe they just made it up." But he knew he wanted it to be true. He wanted there to be bats so big the pigeons feared them. Maybe they were big enough to fight owls too.

With Marina, he dropped from the wall, and skimmed the buildings.

"Maybe we could roost on a rooftop?" he suggested.

"No. Too many pigeons around. There's got to be a tree somewhere."

They rose higher for a better view, and darted out over

a large tree-lined square. In the center was a huge stone building. It didn't look like the others. More like the skeleton of a vast, ancient beast, crouched, its head bent into the earth. At the front, two rough stone towers rose up like pointy shoulder blades. Stretching back was a high-pitched roof, supported by riblike stone arches. Then, at the end of the building rose the highest tower of all, tapering like an animal's bony tail.

And there it was.

Crowning the tower's spire was a metal cross, glinting silver in the city's glow.

"Marina," he said.

With relief, he swept up toward the spire, looking for a place to land—and then in horror, he slammed his wings back, braking furiously.

"Look out!" he screamed.

It was some sort of giant demon, crouched at the base of the spire. Spiked wings were unfolding from its back, and its huge eyes suddenly flashed. Hunched forward as if to lunge, its hellhound jaws were opened wide, spewing saliva.

"There's another one!" shouted Marina, veering away.

Shade did a midair flip and chased after Marina, muscles screaming, waiting for jaws to close around him. One wingbeat and they'd be at his tail, any second now, any second . . . he couldn't stand it any longer. He looked back.

"Wait," he called out to Marina. "Why aren't they moving?"

She circled warily. "Maybe they didn't see us."

"I almost flew into one!" Surely if they were dangerous they'd have struck by now. With his echo vision he took another look. There they were, hunched on the corners of the spire, motionless.

"They're giant bats," he whispered in amazement.

He made a wide pass and saw there were four of the creatures in all, one on each corner, glaring out into the night. Still as stone.

"They're not alive," he shouted back at Marina. He laughed at himself. It was only the city lights that had made their eyes flash. And the saliva drizzling from their open mouths was nothing more than rainwater. Marina flew up beside him.

"But what are they?" she muttered in wonder.

"They're gargoyles," said one of the creatures in a deep echoing voice. "Humans made them."

Shade jolted back; the voice had definitely emanated from a set of gaping jaws.

"Come inside," said the voice again, and Shade recognized it unmistakably as a bat's.

The stone creature's throat, Shade saw now, extended far back into the spire, like a sort of tunnel. He looked at Marina.

"You expect me to go in there?" she said.

"It's the right tower. The cross and everything. And there's definitely a bat inside."

"Don't be afraid," said the bat's voice from deep within the spire.

"Well, that's good enough for me," Marina said sarcastically.

"Look," Shade said. "It's got to be safe. Otherwise my colony wouldn't use it as a landmark, right?"

"After you."

He knew he'd have to go first. He took a deep breath. It wasn't easy flying directly into the dripping jaws of the stone creature. He landed between rows of jagged teeth, half expecting them to snap shut. But they held, frozen, in their fearful grimace.

"Seems okay," he called back to her.

She reluctantly landed beside him, and together they crawled along the trickling stone, farther and farther into the petrified gullet.

"That's right, keep coming," came the voice from the darkness, and Shade, casting a quick sonic glance, caught the outlines of a bat, fluttering out of sight at the tunnel's end.

Overhead, a pipe spewed rainwater onto them, and they hurried past onto the drier stone beyond. The tunnel opened out. Listening intently as his echoes came back to him, Shade saw that they were inside the spire, and the vast space housed several enormous metal objects, like giant pears or flower bulbs, but hollow inside. They were suspended on a system of elaborate ropes, beams, and notched metal wheels.

"My name's Zephyr."

Hanging from a wooden strut was the strangest bat Shade had ever seen. He was of normal size, but his fur was a brilliant white. His wings were pale and completely translucent, so you could see the dark outlines of his forearm and long, spindly fingers. Even the latticework of his veins stood out.

"It has nothing to do with age," the bat explained, as if aware of Shade and Marina's amazement. "I'm an albino—my fur and flesh lack pigment. Even my eyes, when I still had the use of them."

Shade looked into Zephyr's eyes now and saw that they were glazed ghostly white with cataracts.

"Come roost here with me."

Shade and Marina fluttered up and dug their claws into the wood beside Zephyr.

"Those stone creatures," asked Marina, "what are they?"

"They're called gargoyles."

"So that's what the pigeons were talking about!" Shade said. "What are they for?"

"This is a cathedral," Zephyr continued, "a holy place to Humans, constructed long ago. I think they made those gargoyles to frighten away spirits and demons, which only Humans understand. As it turns out, they've served us well here in the city. No bird or beast dares come near the spire. For hundreds of years we've claimed this place as a safe haven, and there has always been a bat sentry posted here, to help travelers in need. And for the past twenty years I have been Keeper of the Spire."

"You live here?" Shade asked.

"Oh yes, all year round."

"Then you must've seen my mother," Shade said excitedly. "With Frieda, and the whole colony!"

"Silverwings, yes," replied the albino bat. "Two nights ago. They didn't stay long, just enough time to take their bearings."

"Told you this was the right place," Shade said to Marina. "Were they all right?" he asked Zephyr.

"You're the bat they lost in the storm."

Shade nodded, surprised. "They told you?"

"They think you're dead."

Shade swallowed. His mother. "Well," he said, "I'm trying to catch up with them. Do you know which way they were going?"

"Don't you have a sound map?"

"Yes, but—I'm not sure I understand it." It would be so much simpler if someone could just explain it so he didn't have to puzzle it out. Two nights ago they'd been here. The gap was widening. They'd have to hurry. He looked hopefully at Zephyr. "If you could tell me—"

"I'm afraid I don't know anything. A colony's sound maps are a great secret. You must know that."

"Oh. Right." He didn't know.

The albino bat frowned and turned his blind gaze on Marina.

"You're not a Silverwing, are you? I can hear the different shape of your wings; even the texture of your fur is different, longer, fuller . . . A Brightwing, am I right?"

"Yes," she said, glancing at Shade in amazement. "But I don't belong to any colony anymore, because—"

"—of your band," Zephyr finished for her, head cocked slightly. "Yes, I can hear it now . . . strange markings . . . I've not heard one quite like that before."

"You've seen others?"

"Of course. May I?" He reached out with one gnarled

claw and touched Marina's band. "You were given it recently, yes?"

"This spring."

"It's newer than any I've seen so far."

Shade looked enviously from Marina to Zephyr. The albino bat seemed more interested in talking to her than him.

"Do you know what it's for?" Marina asked.

"That," Zephyr said, "is a great mystery. It's a link connecting you to the Humans, and—"

"Frieda said it was a sign of the Promise," Shade cut in impatiently. But the albino bat quietly turned his clouded eyes on him, and Shade felt chastened.

"Frieda knows a great deal. But I rather think it's more than a sign. The Humans have a part to play in whatever Nocturna is planning for us. I believe they'll come back to the bats whom they banded. They've been marked for a reason. There's something the Humans want to give them, that's certain, but I think there's something they want from you as well."

Shade looked at his own thin forearms. Naked. No band. Why hadn't he been chosen? And what if he brought Marina back to his colony and suddenly she became the special one. And all those things Frieda had said to him—about him having a brightness—were forgotten. He didn't want to be just a runt again.

"Why are so many bats afraid of the bands?" Marina wanted to know, and she told Zephyr about the Brightwings, and the Graywings they'd met on the way into the city.

"It's right to be wary of the Humans," Zephyr said. "Their customs are mysterious, and they've been known to attack bats, thinking we were pests, or worse, evil spirits, something to be destroyed. And I know for a fact there were bands that killed their wearers. And whether that was the band itself, or the nature of the bat who wore it, no one can say."

"My father had a band," said Shade, "and he discovered something important about it, but—"

"He disappeared this spring in the south, I know," said Zephyr.

"They said owls killed him. We've got to catch up. There're friends of his who might know something, they can tell us where he went . . ."

"Did you know you'd been injured?" Zephyr asked him calmly.

As if on cue, Shade was suddenly conscious of a pain in his left wing. When he looked he could see a tiny puncture in the membrane, slowly oozing dark blood. He felt a little sick.

"One of the pigeons must have pecked you."

"Yeah," said Shade dully, and then: "How'd you know it was the pigeons?"

"Good ears," said Zephyr with a small smile. "I hear a great deal of what goes on in the city skies. And there's been a commotion tonight, let me assure you. A visit from the owl ambassador is not a regular occurrence."

But before Shade could launch a barrage of questions, the albino bat cut him off.

"Now, let's see what we can do about your wound. It's not serious, but it does need some attention. This way."

He led them to a long stone ledge underneath a window, and settled down on all fours among a pile of dried-up leaves. At first Shade thought they'd somehow blown into the tower, but then he realized there were many small neat piles, all different kinds, arranged nearby. Some were so fresh they still had droplets of moisture on them, others so old and wizened they crackled as Zephyr nosed through them. And there were other things too on that cluttered ledge: bright berries, bits of twig, and large bulbous roots with the soil still clinging to them. Insects, long dead and dried up, beetles Shade had certainly never seen, and would have thought twice about eating—scaly armor and horny spikes around the head. There were little pieces of decayed earthworm and grubs and moths.

"What's he got all that stuff for?" Shade whispered suspiciously to Marina.

"I collect them," Zephyr said, obviously overhearing. "There's no need to be suspicious. They're very useful, believe me. Try to keep an open mind, I've been around this earth somewhat longer than you."

Shade grunted, embarrassed. He should've known Zephyr would hear. With his sonic eye he'd seen halfway across the city to the pigeon roost. He could practically read your thoughts.

After a moment the albino bat returned with a berry in one claw and a leaf in another.

"Unfurl your wing," he told Shade. He proceeded to chew the berry, working it over thoroughly in his mouth.

"What're you doing?" Shade asked.

Without answering, Zephyr leaned over Shade's wound and drizzled the finely mulched berry juice onto it. It stung and Shade flinched.

"Hey!"

"This will prevent an infection from spreading through your wing. And it will heal faster." Zephyr gently spread the oily fluid with his tongue.

"A berry does all that?" Marina asked.

"It's a common enough potion," said Zephyr. "Now, sleep is the best thing for you."

"No," said Shade, "we can't stay. I mean, we need to get going, we've lost so much time." But he felt exhausted, and now the rip in his wing was beginning to hurt, sending sharp jabs into his shoulder.

"Believe me, Silverwing, you need the sleep," said Zephyr. "And you couldn't find the route you need right now, even if you wanted to."

Shade didn't understand. He was about to ask him to explain, but Zephyr had already taken a very small nibble of the leaf he'd carried over. This one had a distinctive shape and dark veins, and Shade couldn't remember ever having seen it before. But then, he'd never paid much attention to the shapes of leaves. You couldn't eat them—at least that's what he'd thought before now.

"Open your mouth," he told Shade.

Shade hesitated.

With a hint of impatience Zephyr said, "It will help you sleep."

Reluctantly, Shade opened his jaws, wincing as the albino bat drizzled the leaf juice down his throat. At least it didn't taste terrible—in fact, it had almost no taste at all.

"You should sleep on all fours tonight, with the wing spread flat."

"They were going to peck off our wings," he told Zephyr, not without pride. "They said giant bats killed two of their soldiers earlier tonight."

"Yes, I overheard one of the owl guards."

"And they're closing the skies!" Shade said, remembering in a rush. How stupid: He should've told Zephyr all this earlier. It was important. But with all the other new things, the gargoyles and meeting an albino bat, and finding the right tower—

"I know about the closed skies too," Zephyr told him gently.

"Oh, right," said Shade. He yawned, then perked up again. "There're no bats that big really, are there?"

"Get some sleep," Zephyr told him. "We'll talk more tomorrow night."

Already Shade could feel a heavy, delicious warmth spreading through his body, and a wonderful sense of safety overtook him. That sense of being home, a place like Tree Haven, close to his mother. He looked groggily at Marina.

"I think, probably, I'll just have a quick nap—"

The inside of the tower seemed to become very dark—even his sound vision faltered, silvery lines fading—and then pure, silent blackness swallowed him up.

*  *  *

Goth landed beside Throbb on a ledge in the metal shaft. Foul fumes rose up from the darkness below, but at least they were warm. It was the best roost he could find in the rooftops of this cursed city. He didn't know much about Human buildings, and he hadn't had much time before the sun came up.

The sun. That at least had shown him where east was, and from there he could guess at south. But he knew he'd need more than that to stay on course for a whole night.

He'd have to understand these new northern stars.

"We need a guide," he said to Throbb. "Someone to show us how to read the sky—that's the only way to get back home. We have to find a bat."

# STAR MAP

Shade opened his eyes, as if he'd just blinked, and saw Zephyr looking down at him.

"Oh," he said, "I thought I'd fallen asleep."

The albino bat laughed. "You did. You slept through the whole day. The sun's just gone down."

Shade frowned. It seemed he'd just closed his eyes, but he certainly felt refreshed and alert. He remembered the tear in his wing and looked: The berry oil had formed a pale opaque film over it, and the pain was now only a dim ache.

"I guess that plant stuff really works," he said, tentatively flexing his wing. "Where's Marina?"

"Down in the cathedral. She wanted to look at the Humans." Zephyr pointed the way to a wide shaft in the center of the floor.

"What do they do down there?" Shade asked a little uncertainly. He'd never seen a Human.

"They meet here in the evenings sometimes. They talk and sing. I believe they pray as well. Go see, if you like."

Shade lit from the stone ledge where he'd slept, and circled the spire several times to test his wing. A little stiff, and sore on the downstroke, but not bad at all. He cautiously spiraled down the shaft and felt like he'd entered the belly of a giant beast.

Never had he been inside such a colossal space. Huge pillars stretched from the floor to the vaulted ceiling. High windows glinted darkly in the walls. Cold seeped across his wings. Suspended above the floor on long chains were lights in circular metal holders. He thought of the Promise: that ring of light, and felt impatient. There was so much he wanted to know.

Beneath the lights were Humans, sitting in neat rows, all facing a raised platform on which stood a single male in robes. Shade kept his distance up near the rafters, shooting out quick tendrils of sound.

So this is what they looked like.

Of course they'd been described to him by his mother, and there were always stories going around. But they were huge, much taller than he expected. Their limbs were thick and powerful. What was it like, he wondered, not to fear anything? To never be scanning the horizon all the time, even when you ate, making sure nothing was sneaking up on you.

They were wingless, of course. He stared at their backs and shoulders quite a long time, just to make sure. He felt a quick pang of pity. How horrible, to be stuck on the ground your whole life, while other creatures got to soar above you. He couldn't imagine not flying. He supposed he shouldn't feel sorry for them, though. Maybe they didn't mind. Anyway, he remembered Frieda once saying they had metal machines that let them fly. They had machines for practically everything it seemed. They were geniuses.

He found Marina intently watching the Humans. She didn't look at him as he roosted beside her.

"I've never seen so many all in one place," she breathed, a look of anticipation on her face. As if something wonderful was about to happen.

Suddenly the Humans all stood, and began speaking in unison, their deep slow voices filling the cathedral. What were they saying? Strange music spiraled crazily from a set of pipes high in a loft. Shade wished he understood what it all meant. The Humans' intense concentration charged the air, and Shade's fur lifted.

"I want to go to them," Marina said, and Shade was stirred by the longing in her face. He twitched his nose awkwardly. He didn't feel her passion, and it bothered him. The band—it was all to do with the band, and he didn't have one.

"After my colony left me," she said, "I was always looking for the two Humans who banded me. Once I thought I saw them. It was stupid, I mean, it's not as if I got a good look at them. But I flew toward them anyway, and it was just like with the bats. They were scared. They waved their arms, and shouted, and covered their faces." She gave a quick laugh. "Not exactly overjoyed to see me."

"Not all Humans are the same," Zephyr said, fluttering down to them. "The ones who give the bands will not fear you."

"If we ever find them," said Marina.

The Humans stopped talking and stood in silence.

"Are they praying now?" Shade asked Zephyr.

"I think so."

It was baffling. What did they have to pray for? Didn't they already have everything they needed?

"They're fighting a war of their own, you know," Zephyr said.

Shade looked at him in amazement. "With the beasts? I suppose it is, the birds are too small. Apes? Is it apes, or maybe the wolves? I've heard stories about how strong—"

"It's with one another, as far as I can gather."

Humans fighting Humans—it was mind-boggling. "Why?"

"That I don't know. The fighting takes place far away. But that needn't concern you now. What does is the pigeons. They're looking for you."

"Here?"

"Oh, don't worry. They don't dare land on the cathedral.

They seem more afraid of the gargoyles than ever."

"They come to life, that's what some of them think," Shade said.

"It was real bats who killed those two soldiers last night."

"Who are they?"

"I don't know them." The albino bat seemed troubled. "I've only heard them as they cross the city. They're strangers, and I don't think they've been here long. But they've set something fearful in motion."

Shade knew he meant the owls closing the skies. And he was right: That spelled danger for every single bat alive.

"But why did the bats attack?" asked Marina.

"Why shouldn't they?" Shade said with a snort. "Look what the pigeons nearly did to us. And the owls, burning down our roost. Killing my father. They've got it coming."

"You may be right," said Zephyr. "But this could turn into a war, and war is nothing to hope for."

Shade grunted. But what if war was the only way? Zephyr couldn't know everything. Frieda said they couldn't win against the birds, but what about these two giant bats? If there were enough of them . . .

"Well, I'll feel a whole lot better when we put the city behind us," said Marina. "So, just as soon as boy wonder here figures out where we're going . . . " She looked at Shade expectantly.

He sighed. He knew he'd found the right tower, and the cross matched perfectly. But he also knew somehow it wasn't enough. There was one more piece of the puzzle, and without it, he had nothing.

From beyond the cathedral's stone walls came a muted clang, and Shade's ears pricked.

*Bong* . . .

Then another:

*Bong* . . .

It was the same sound they'd heard last night from the

pigeons' tower. The wrong tower, but still, Shade was sure this was the sound from his mother's map.

"What's that for?" he asked Zephyr urgently.

"It's how the Humans measure time. One clang for every hour."

*Bong . . . bong . . .*

He summoned up his mother's sound map: that clanging noise . . . how many times had it sounded in his mind? Seven? Yes, definitely seven. And last night he'd only heard three.

*Bong, bong*—that made six so far. . . .

Shade waited breathlessly.

And then came a final:

*Bong.*

Seven bongs. This was the right time. And this tower was the right place. In his mind, the spire and the cross beckoned to him with new urgency.

"Come on!" he yelled to Marina.

Without explaining, he beat his way back up the shaft into the spire, and then out through a gargoyle's throat. He flew through the gaping jaws and swirled to the very top of the spire. Marina and Zephyr weren't far behind.

"I think I understand!" he told Marina. "My mother gave me the time, and the place I'm supposed to be, so I can chart our new course by the stars!"

Shade hung upside down from the horizontal bar of the cross. Lucky it was a clear night: Stars were strewn across the sky. His mother's sound map was very precise. He had to be in the very center of the cross. He shuffled over. A circle of hollow metal ringed the junction. A cross inside a circle. He recognized the image now!

Within the circle the heavens were divided into four quadrants.

"So what are we looking for?" he heard Marina ask.

A string of stars drifted through three of the quadrants. Which one did he want? He conjured up the sound map once more.

Stars.

The sky divided into four.

One star flaring brighter than all the others, surging toward him.

The top right quadrant!

That's where he should look.

And there it was, right where his mother had sung it— a bright star. Their star.

"I've got it!" he shouted, pointing with his wingtip. "All we've got to do is fly straight for it! Easy, huh?"

"Following stars is a tricky business," said Zephyr. "They move you know."

"They do?" Of course they did. Stupid. He knew that, but had forgotten in all the excitement. The stars weren't simply fixed in the sky. His mother explained how they moved around in a circle every night, finishing where they started. But that was all he knew. He hadn't learned star navigation yet.

"I think I can handle it," said Marina.

Shade grimaced. He'd cracked the puzzle, and now Marina got to do the rest.

"We'll have to take our bearings the same time every night," she said, glancing at the glow on the west horizon. "Just a bit after sundown. We won't have that bonging sound to tell us once we leave the city."

"You'll have to learn to measure time in your head," Zephyr told them. "Your bodies know very well how much time has passed with each wingbeat. The stars move at a fixed rate: Once you know that, you'll be able to check your course throughout the night, using that same star as a guide."

"Oh, sure, I get it now," said Shade breezily. He gazed through the cross. It seemed awfully difficult.

"You'll manage," said the Keeper of the Spire, "between the two of you."

Shade looked out across the city, and shivered in the sharp air. It wasn't safe anymore, the night. The pigeons would be searching for him and Marina. The thought of setting out again filled him with weariness. Who knew how long it would be before they caught up with the others? He wished, for a moment, he could simply stay here at the spire with Zephyr. It wouldn't be so bad. It was safe, and obviously warm enough through the winter. And they were sure to learn an awful lot. Zephyr seemed to know almost as much as Frieda . . .

"You'd best set off now, Silverwing," Zephyr said gently.

"Yes," said Shade gratefully. Of course he had to keep going.

"Follow that star of yours," Zephyr told him, and tilted his chin up so he seemed to be looking right at it.

"You can *see* it?" Shade asked.

"With my ears," replied the old bat simply.

Shade whistled in disbelief. How could you hear the stars? It was impossible! They were too far away.

"When you lose one sense, you develop your others many times over," Zephyr said. "And how do you know you couldn't hear the stars, if only you paid enough attention to them. It's just a question of practice and perseverance."

"I suppose," said Shade. He made a mental note to try to listen harder to things.

"I see things inside here too," said the albino bat, gesturing with a white claw to his head.

"Like what?" said Marina.

"The past, the future. It's all a question of echoes. If you listen you can still hear the reverberations of things just happened, just a second ago, an hour ago. If you listen very hard indeed, you can still hear things that happened last winter, or ten winters ago, as if they were right before your eyes. It's the same with the future. Everything has a sound, and it's just a matter of time before it reaches you; but if you have very good hearing, you can hear it coming from a long way off."

"Can you see if we catch up with the colony?" Shade asked impulsively. How could he not ask?

The albino bat hunched over slightly, and froze in intense concentration. His tall pointed ears reached upward, flared wide. Then, with a sigh, he spread his pale wings, as if they would somehow help him trap sound.

As Shade watched silently, the underside of his wings seemed to darken. Shade blinked, wondering if his eyes were playing tricks on him, maybe the paleness of Zephyr's flesh was somehow weirdly reflecting the sky. But the wings definitely seemed to be turning black and then sparkling when—

Zephyr suddenly wrapped them over his head, cloaking himself. "It will be like all journeys, difficult, and not what you expect." His voice sounded distant, uncertain. "You'll meet an unexpected ally, but beware of metal on wings . . . and . . . you will find Hibernaculum—"

Shade's heart leaped, but Zephyr's voice was far from joyous as he continued.

"—but others are searching for it too, powerful forces, and I can't see who will reach it first, or whether what they bring is good or bad . . . And your father, Cassiel . . ."

"What?" Shade exclaimed. "What about him?"

The albino bat hesitated a moment before saying: "He's alive."

Zephyr stopped and his head reappeared. He quickly folded his wings back. "I can't hear any more. The echoes are so faint and confused."

"But couldn't you see where—"

The albino bat shook his head regretfully. "Only that he's far away."

"Alive," Shade muttered in amazement. Deep in his heart he'd always hoped it was true. His mother and Frieda were wrong. Cassiel had just disappeared, but where? He looked restlessly into the sky.

"So, good-bye," Zephyr said. "And good luck."

"Thank you," Shade said. He lit from the spire, circling

with Marina. "And thanks for fixing my wing too. And everything else."

"Good-bye," called Marina over her wing.

They flew high, eager to get clear of the rooftops, and the pigeons that roosted there. Marina suggested they split up the sky between them, to make sure they didn't miss anything. Shade tried to calm his mind. His father, alive . . . Impossible as it was, he knew he had to concentrate. He forced all his senses together as one. He sniffed, he listened, he scanned the night for any sign of birds.

When they were far above the highest towers, and the whole glorious, gleaming city was spread before them, they leveled off. Shade found his guiding star and pointed his nose toward it.

"Did you see the underside of Zephyr's wings?" he asked hesitantly.

"I was wondering if it was just a thing with the light," Marina said eagerly.

"Me too."

"But—"

"I don't think it was, was it?" he asked.

There was a silence.

"You saw it too, didn't you?" Marina asked.

Shade nodded. "His wings got dark underneath."

"Yes," she said. "They were black as night—and they were filled with stars."

Goth looked down over the glittering lights. He'd been circling with Throbb for over an hour now, gradually spiraling out toward the city's edges, searching for bats. They'd seen none. Did bats even exist this far north? It was a sickening thought. What if they didn't? How would he find a guide? How would he get home?

He'd had a dream just before sunset. He was back in the jungle, glorying in the heat, and suddenly, all around him were hundreds of bats, not his own kind, but small bats, the smallest he'd ever seen, flying joyful circles around him, chanting his name. What are they doing here, he wondered, but he was overcome with a feeling of triumph. Until the giant trees and vines and ferns of the jungle suddenly toppled over, and all around were walls, Human walls, and behind one of them stood the Man, smiling at him.

Goth shook his head. It was rare for him to dream, and he'd learned that it was always important, a way for Zotz to speak to him. What did it mean?

"Look!" Throbb hissed. "Down there."

Goth peered down through the sky and smiled with relief.

Bats.

# CLOSED SKIES

"Did you hear that?"

"What?" Marina asked.

"Wingbeats." Shade looked back over his wing, sweeping the sky with his eyes and echo vision. Nothing.

They'd finally reached the outskirts of the city, and Shade was exhausted. He couldn't believe how lucky they'd been. Twice they'd seen a distant squad of pigeons patrolling rooftops, and once he'd spotted an owl sentry silhouetted against the rising moon. But they'd passed unnoticed. Still, he couldn't shake the feeling they were being followed. The moonlight made him nervous. It lit the silver in his fur, and Marina, at times, positively glowed.

At least they were far away from the ocean now. And he could smell trees and fields up ahead, hear their familiar outlines. He knew what to stay away from here, where he could eat, where he could hide.

"I still can't believe my father's alive," he said. "Where though?"

"He disappeared around Hibernaculum, right? That's where you start looking."

"What if the owls have him?" Shade had heard terrible stories about owls using bats as slaves, to build nests, hollow out trees—and then eating them.

Marina shook her head. Shade knew even if they found him in time, it would be almost impossible to rescue him from an owl nest.

"Maybe he's with the Humans," Marina said hopefully.

Shade smiled. It was a comforting thought. But why wouldn't his father have come to tell Ariel and the others—to tell *him*. He wouldn't just desert them all, keep the secrets to himself?

The owl plunged from behind, silent wings spread, and it was only the pungent odor that made Shade whirl just in time. He cried out, and flipped to the side—fast enough to escape the claws, but not the wings. The blow sent him spinning down to the trees, stunned. He hit a branch, the impact softened by dried leaves, and sunk his claws into the wood so he wouldn't slip off.

Enormous eyes bore down on him. He scrambled to get out of the way as the owl battered the branch with its wings. He saw Marina hurl herself against the bird's back, and sink her claws and teeth into the dense feathers.

The owl shrieked in fury, swiveled its immense head, and stabbed at Marina with its hooked beak. She jerked clear, and the owl slapped her off with its wing.

And turned back to Shade. All he could see were those flat moonlike eyes—and then something big and dark struck the bird from the side, and clung. It was as if part of the night sky had torn loose and lashed down. The owl bellowed in agony. Shade saw powerful black wings, then claws, and a set of jaws opening and clamping down on the owl's neck. There was a horrible cracking noise.

It was a bat.

The bat opened his jaws and the owl slumped lifeless, its wings tangled in the branches. He looked at Shade.

"Are you all right?"

Shade nodded. "Thank you," he whispered, his throat dry. He felt extraordinarily small. This bat was at least four times his size. As if the stone gargoyles really had come to life. The similarity was unsettling. The face was more beast than bat, with a long snout, spattered with blood, large eyes, and a strange flared nose that spiked upward.

A second huge bat, wings spanning at least three feet across, circled overhead.

"My name's Goth," said the first bat. "And that," he said, with a dismissive flick of his head, "is my companion, Throbb."

"I'm Shade, and—" He broke off and looked around in alarm. "Marina!"

"I'm here," she said, fluttering over and glancing warily at Goth and Throbb. "You okay, Shade?"

"They saved my life," he said excitedly, turning to Goth. "You're from the city, aren't you? You're the ones who killed the pigeons."

"How did you know that?"

"Because they caught us," Marina said, "and wanted to know who you were."

"Did they attack you?" Shade asked.

The giant bat laughed. "Pigeons? No. We were hungry." He leaned over the body of the owl and ripped a hunk of flesh from its chest.

Shade flinched in surprise.

"You're not meat-eaters," Goth said with interest, after swallowing the owl flesh in one gulp.

"No."

"You're welcome to try some."

"No, thank you." The smell was repulsive, heavy with blood, and Shade saw Marina take a few steps away from the owl's body.

"Where we come from, many are meat-eaters," Goth explained. "I'm sorry if it alarms you."

"Where *do* you come from?" Marina asked.

"The jungle. If it weren't for the Humans, we'd be there now. We escaped just last night. Look." He pulled back his wing, and the thick black metal band around his forearm caught the moonlight. Shade sucked in his breath, and glanced up at Throbb, still flying above them. A band glinted darkly on his forearm too.

"Escaped?" Marina asked, frowning. "I don't understand."

"You've been their prisoner too, I see," Goth remarked, nodding at her band.

"No. They didn't imprison me. They gave me the band, and let me go, but—"

"They didn't take you to the false jungle?"

Shade looked at Marina, who shook her head, dumbfounded.

As Goth ate, he told them about being captured by the Humans, and the month he spent in their jungle prison. Shade listened intently as the giant bat described how the Humans had flashed lights in his face, stuck him with darts.

"But why would the Humans do that?" Marina asked.

"I think they were studying us. They want our powers of flight, and our night vision. They band us to mark us as their prisoners."

"No," Marina said, so softly Shade almost didn't hear.

He didn't know what to think. Everything Goth said flew in the face of what he'd been told. That the band was a sign of the Promise, a link between bats and Humans, that the Humans would somehow help them. Could Frieda and Zephyr . . . and his father . . . could they all be wrong? He felt sick.

"They didn't take me prisoner," Marina said stubbornly.

Goth shrugged. "They're not our friends, the Humans. And they will be punished," he added darkly.

Three mournful hoots floated through the night air.

"What was that?" asked Goth, his crest bristling.

"More owls," Shade told him. "They're calling for their sentry. They'll come if they don't hear back from him. We should get moving. Which way are you going?"

"We don't know. We want to go south to the jungle, but we're not familiar with these stars of yours."

"You come from a place with different stars?" Shade asked.

"That's right. Brighter, and more numerous than these."

Shade turned to Marina, incredulous. No one had ever told him about a jungle world, where the bats ate meat, and the sky contained a different set of stars. Did Frieda or Zephyr even know about such a place?

"Is it always so cold here?" Throbb asked with a shudder.

"Just in winter."

"Winter," said Throbb, as if pronouncing a new word.

Shade was surprised. Maybe where they came from, they didn't have winter. He began to feel useful.

"We're migrating," he explained. "Every winter we go south to find a warmer place to hibernate."

"Hibernate?" said Goth.

"A long sleep."

"How long?"

"Months." He was glad that someone shared his amazement at the idea of hibernation. "That's all we do, sleep and sleep until it gets warmer."

"Well, how unusual," said Goth with a laugh. "Bats that sleep for months on end. What strange customs you have in the north." He looked up at the sky. "But you can read these stars, can you?"

"We're going south too," Shade said, and then added impulsively, "come with us. We're trying to catch up with my colony. I'm sure Frieda could tell you how to get back to the jungle."

Goth turned to him and smiled gratefully.

"That's very generous of you."

"I don't like them," Marina said. She and Shade were alone, hunting the riverbank for insects.

Shade caught a snout beetle and cracked the shell.

"Well, I feel a lot safer traveling with them."

There was a strangled squeal from the forest floor, and they both saw Goth fly out of the trees with a rat thrashing in his jaws.

"They're eating half the forest," Marina said. "It doesn't bother you they're meat-eaters?"

"They're from the jungle," he said impatiently. "Everything's different there. Probably why they're so big," he mumbled. It made sense, all that heavy meat. He wondered, if he were to . . . he grimaced, remembering the pungent smell of owl. "What does it matter what they eat? We eat insects, they eat other animals. You expect me to be sad about that owl? This is the second owl that's wanted to eat me, and they were quite happy about it, and I've heard stories about how owls eat you, pulling out your insides while you're still alive."

"Well, just remember, it's your two friends who got the skies closed down. And every time they kill something, a pigeon or an owl or a rat, the birds and beasts are going to want revenge. And that's bad news for us, and any other bat out there."

He knew she was right, and it made him angry. He thought of the rat Goth had just killed. He hoped Goth had been careful, picked a straggler.

"Look, the owls started it, not us. They can't just close down the night skies."

"I just don't like them," Marina said again. "I don't trust them."

"Remember what Zephyr said about meeting an unexpected ally?"

"You think that's Goth?" She rustled her wings. "He also said that stuff about beware of metal under wings. Maybe that means Goth."

"You've got metal under your wings too."

"I'd thought of that already, believe me."

"You don't like what they said about the bands, do you?"

"Do you?" she demanded.

"No. But . . ."

"What?"

"Doesn't mean it's not true."

"They didn't imprison me. They didn't put me in a room and jab me with darts and study me. I just can't believe Humans are as bad as they say."

"Zephyr did say they wanted something from us . . ."

"But also that there was something they wanted to give us," Marina insisted.

"I don't know." His head was beginning to ache.

"What about your elder, Frieda? What about Zephyr? And your own father? You think they were all wrong?"

"I don't—I just don't know!"

"So you're saying my colony was right all along. Humans are our enemies—"

"I didn't say that, Marina—"

"And here I thought maybe the band meant something." She tapped it sharply against his head. "But all it means is I'm a prisoner. That's it. No secret anymore. I guess I don't need to come any farther, do I?"

An awkward silence fell between them.

"I want to go back," she said quietly.

"What?"

"I want to go back."

"To the island?"

"To the city. I want to find this fake jungle."

"Are you crazy? What about the pigeons? The owls? It's not safe. And even if you did find this place, how do you know . . ." he sighed. "How do you know they won't hurt you."

"How do you know your father's not there?"

Shade felt his breath knocked out of him. He stared at Marina. It hadn't even occurred to him. But no. He shook his head in relief. "Zephyr said he was far away. Remember?"

Marina sighed. "Let's leave Goth and Throbb . . ."

"We need them," he said bluntly. "We weren't two

hours out of the city when we got hit by that owl. You think we can make it on our own?"

Marina was silent.

"I want to know what it all means too." He ignored her doubtful snort. "I really do. But let's just catch up with my colony, and then we can talk to Frieda and the other banded bats and maybe we'll get more answers."

"You're pretty impressed by these two, aren't you?"

She'd caught him by surprise. "Well . . ."

"Big like you always wanted to be?" There was a taunting hook to her voice.

"Maybe," he said, face burning. "So what?"

"I wish you hadn't asked them to join us."

"Listen," he said. "We're safe with them. And what if there is a war? What if that's what Nocturna meant? And even my father said we had to wait for something before we'd be free. Maybe this is it."

"What d'you mean?"

"Goth and Throbb. There're others like them in the jungle, right? Maybe we can convince them to join us. Make a big army." His heart whirred furiously with excitement. "You saw the way Goth killed the owl. It was easy for him. I mean just look at them, they're natural warriors. If we had their help, we could fight them once and for all—all the pigeons and the owls and anyone else. Everyone who wanted to keep us banished. And I know we could beat them."

# Dark Allies

Goth ripped another hunk from his squirrel and chewed thoughtfully. He looked up at the sky. This was the second night he'd spent with Shade and Marina, and he was beginning to recognize a few of these stars now. It wouldn't be long before he could navigate by himself, and then he could make a quick meal of these two little bats.

Still, they were useful in other ways. He didn't understand the trees here, some with spindly leafless branches, others with sharp prickly needles. It was Marina who'd found a place for them to roost last night, in a deserted woodpecker's hole. And Shade had shown him how to drink from the stream, by breaking through the frozen water. He called it ice. Ice. Never had he seen such a horrific thing. It was painful to touch, the cold seeping into him with a shock. He ruffled his wings and closed them tighter around his body. But the wind cut through anyway. The sooner he was free of this northern wasteland the better.

Throbb landed beside him with a sparrow in his jaws.

"I want bat," he whined.

"Not yet," Goth growled. "Wait. You'll get bat soon enough. Have some self-discipline, and remember," he added ominously, looking Throbb right in the eye, "I like bat too."

Throbb shuffled back a few inches and ate his sparrow sullenly. "Who's this Nocturna they keep talking about?"

Goth used a claw to pick out some meat between his teeth. "Some pathetic little religion, I suppose." Shade had told him all about it: the battle between birds and beasts, the banishment, and this wonderful Promise. It was all ridiculous, but he said nothing, preferring to keep Zotz, the one true bat god, secret for the time being.

"Even if Nocturna does exist," he said derisively, "she can't be very powerful—just look at the puny creatures she rules over."

Throbb hacked out a laugh, spitting up some gristle and bones at the same time.

They really were pitiful creatures, Goth thought. They couldn't even defend themselves against pigeons. The owls, he'd admit, were somewhat more formidable—fighting more than two at a time would be a challenge. Still, these bats lived in total fear of them, afraid to show their faces during the day, and now even at night, according to Shade.

Goth smiled, pleased. It seemed he'd started a war.

And they needed him, these two bats. Shade wanted him to meet the leaders of his colony. Of course Goth had willingly agreed, knowing he'd be long gone by then. Once he could fly south alone, he certainly wouldn't need the help of some mangy Silverwing elder.

Unless . . .

The thought slid into his head like a snake's tongue. Unless Zotz meant for him to meet the Silverwing colony. Unless there was a design behind his capture by Humans in the jungle. It made sense. Why would Zotz have let the Humans bring him north, if not for a purpose?

The dream. Hundreds upon hundreds of Silverwings flying around him in the jungle. And how did they get there? They got there, a voice inside his head told him, because you brought them there.

\* \* \*

"In the jungle," Goth was saying, "it's never cold. The heat hangs in the air like rain. The landscape is lush, not like this rocky forest below us, but bright with flowers and plants and fruits, the likes of which you've never seen. And the insects there are so succulent—three or four would be enough to feed you for an entire night."

Shade listened, rapt, as they flew through the cold sky. It was not the beetles Goth described, but the warmth that made his mouth water. Waking this evening, he'd been startled to find a faint dusting of frost on his outer wing tips, and he'd beaten it off anxiously.

This was the third night they'd spent with Goth and Throbb, and they were still navigating by the cathedral star. He wondered how long it would be before they caught up with the other Silverwings. The whole world was glazed with frost, the naked tree branches glinting silver. The sound of insects had dulled over the past nights, and hunting was becoming more difficult. Fewer living things came out at night now. From time to time he'd spotted huge flocks of birds in the distance, making their own migration south. So far, though, there'd been no sign of any other bat colonies, and this worried him.

"There's a sheltered ledge over there," Marina said, pointing to a rocky hillside. "We should probably find a roost, and then we'll have about an hour to feed."

Shade shivered and looked to the east. He hated stopping, always felt like he was losing time. But at least the sun meant it would be a little warmer soon. His ears ached, and his feet felt numb.

"How many bats are there in your colony?" he asked Goth as they circled the ledge, checking for roosts.

"Millions."

Millions. It was hard enough to imagine two giant bats, much less millions.

"There's probably not much in the sky you're afraid of," Shade said enviously.

"Nothing," Goth told him. "The vulture and hawk are

the only birds of any strength, but they don't dare attack us."

Shade wondered what it would be like not to be afraid. He'd never know: He was a runt. Practically everything in the sky was bigger than him. But if he could convince Goth and Throbb to join them . . . maybe that would count for something.

He'd agonized over how to ask them, and given up the whole idea more than once. What did he know? Who was he to ask these giant bats to join their fight? Maybe he should leave it all to Frieda or the other elders.

Marina found a tunnel in the stone face, big enough for Goth and Throbb to fit through. Inside, it was dry and protected from the wind, and small enough so their body heat would quickly warm it up. Shade scanned the floor intently.

"What're you doing?" Goth asked.

"Checking for owl pellets. To make sure they haven't been nesting here." Marina had taught him how to do it. Owls swallowed their prey whole; they didn't chew, and their pellets contained all the bones and teeth of whatever they'd eaten. He was afraid one night he'd find a part of a bat's wing-fingers or jawbone. This place was clean, however.

"You live in constant fear of them, don't you," Goth said.

"We're too small to fight them."

"But if five of you attacked one . . ."

Shade had never thought of that. "Maybe," he said.

"We can't allow our bat brothers and sisters to be treated this way," Goth said fiercely, looking at Shade, and at first Shade thought Goth was angry with him, thinking him a coward. He looked at the floor.

"Come with us to the jungle," Goth said, "you and all your colony, and I'll call upon my family for help."

"You will?" It was more than Shade could have hoped for.

"We can muster an army, and return to the north to fight the owls."

"You'll really fight with us?"

"It would be a great honor to help you return to the light of day, just like Nocturna promised."

"All without the Humans' help?" Marina asked.

Shade looked at her in surprise. She'd gone almost the whole night without saying a word. He knew she was angry, at Goth, and at him. She was staring at Goth belligerently.

"I wouldn't count on any help from Humans," Goth snorted. "They're more interested in imprisoning us than setting us free."

Shade felt Marina staring hard at him, but he couldn't meet her gaze. The Humans . . . he just didn't know what to think about them now. They seemed unreliable. Marina thought they were good; Goth and Throbb thought they were evil. As for the bands, there were ones like Frieda's, and others that burned bats alive. How could they count on Humans?

"Maybe Goth's right," he said, still avoiding Marina's eyes. "Maybe the Humans aren't going to help us."

"What do you know?" she snapped bitterly. "You aren't even banded."

Shade looked at her, stung.

"Maybe I'm not, but—"

"No. You don't know what it was like. How it felt. It was special, I don't care what any of you say. It means something." She paused. "And your father thought so too, Shade."

He was aware of Goth, watching him intently.

"I know what my father thought," he said coldly. "Maybe he was wrong."

"So you're just going to give up on him? Go off to the jungle without looking for him?"

"Of course I'll look for him—"

"So it's just me you're giving up on."

Before he could even fumble for words, she flew out from the stone hollow into the night.

"Marina!" he shouted, and was about to dart after her, but Goth spread one of his massive wings.

"Don't worry. She'll be back. Let her calm down."

"I didn't want to hurt her feelings."

"You didn't. She's put too much hope on these bands. Now she feels angry and foolish. She'll get over it."

"Yeah," said Shade, looking after her. He should have felt deliriously happy, knowing that Goth and Throbb were going to help him form an army. But he felt a dead-weight of disappointment in his stomach.

"We know the stars well enough by now," Throbb said. "What use are the bats? Let's eat them."

"Keep your voice down," Goth hissed, looking across the treetops to where Shade foraged alone for insects. He turned back to Throbb. "You'll do as I say, when I say. Without me you'd still be back in that prison, eating those watery little mice. Remember that."

He hadn't told Throbb about his plan, and he wouldn't. Everything had become so clear to him, once he'd managed to unlock the dream's meaning.

He would travel with Shade and Marina until they met the Silverwings. Then, he would convince them to come to the jungle, thinking they would raise an army.

But once they reached his homeland, all the Silverwings would become slaves to his family. Year after year they would breed, creating an endless supply of living bat flesh for them to devour.

They would become eternal sacrificial offerings to Zotz—who had sent his servant Goth to the north to prove himself, and bring the Silverwings to the jungle.

Shade hadn't suspected his purpose; it had been so easy. The Silverwing was spirited, yes, and intelligent, but he was also desperate for glory—as if he could ever have it, the scrawny little thing.

But Marina . . . he was more worried about her: She doubted them, he could tell. It seemed like Shade was safely on his side now, but he wondered how loyal he would be to his Brightwing companion. He couldn't afford to lose Shade, and if she should sway him . . .

He turned to Throbb.

"You want bat so badly? Find the Brightwing and kill her."

"Marina!"

Shade was getting worried now. He'd fed alone for half an hour, and still she hadn't come back. She shouldn't be off alone, not now of all times. There might be owl sentries nearby, a clutch of crows . . .

He flew past the stone ledge where they'd found a roost. He hadn't seen Goth or Throbb either. Panic fluttered through him. Had a squadron of owls struck without him knowing? Taken all of them?

He wanted to shout out, but knew that would only mark him if there were owls nearby. He began a wide circle around the roost, staying high enough above the trees, but peering down into them with his echo vision. He finished his first circle and started again, wider.

In the branches of an oak he spotted Throbb, hunched over, his back to him. With relief he flew down closer and could hear the raw, sticky sounds of feeding, of things being wrenched and chewed. Splayed to one side of Throbb's shoulders and head, he could make out the outline of a lifeless wing.

His usual revulsion suddenly gave way to horror. His echo vision flared at the edges, and he was seized with a terrible weakness, afraid he might faint.

There were no feathers on that wing.

It was fringed with bright fur, leathery, with the ridges of long fingers beneath the surface.

Throbb was eating a Brightwing bat.

# ESCAPE

Shade wheeled, and dived into the trees, but he was too late.

"Shade? Is that you? Shade!"

Crouched in his hiding place, he could see Throbb, turning slowly, seeking him out with beams of sound. The Brightwing's head fell from his jaws and lolled to one side, so Shade could see the face. He almost cried out in relief. Not Marina. He had to find her. He released his grip, opened his wings, and flew.

"Shade!"

He'd stick below the tree line. Throbb's wings were too wide to follow him. Through the tight weave of foliage he flashed, flipping from side to side, almost over onto his back sometimes, to avoid getting impaled on a pointy twig, or dashing himself against a trunk.

Overhead, he could hear Throbb curse, then send sound piercing down through the leaves and branches, trying to get a fix on him. Wings pulled tight, Shade flew headlong, trying to keep track of Throbb's position. Silently, not grazing even a single leaf, he banked tightly, darting back the way he'd come. Then, twice more he made quick changes in direction, until he could no longer hear Throbb's crackling wingbeats above him.

He peered up through the leaves, and pieced together a

bit of the sky. Where would she be? It was almost dawn, she couldn't stay out much longer.

She'd go back to the roost.

Choking for breath, he burst from the cover of the trees and streaked toward the stone hollow. He sent out a quick spray of sound. No sign of Goth—he must still be out hunting. But he pulled back from the entrance at the last moment, circling. What if Throbb had beaten him back? What if he was waiting inside?

"Marina?" he called out quietly.

"In here," came her voice from the roost.

He was lucky. He shot through the tunnel and into the stone hollow. There she was, grooming her wings, and he was so grateful to see her, even though she looked up at him coldly, still angry.

"Marina, we've got to—" His flesh crawled.

Goth was perched silently at the back of the hollow, still gnawing on a bone. It seemed impossible to him that he'd felt safe with this bat, just hours ago. Now, the sight of him chewing made him sick to his stomach. Meat-eater. Bat-eater.

"Got to what?" Goth asked.

Shade forced himself to land, take a few deep breaths. He was covered with sweat and dust. "Oh, I was going to tell Marina she should come see this big icicle near the stream."

"I'm tired," Marina said with a yawn. "And I've seen icicles before, Shade."

"Not one this big." He stared at her, and she looked back at him strangely before giving a quick nod.

"All right, all right, show me this icicle. Then let's get some sleep."

"Okay. We won't be long," he told Goth.

"I'll come too."

Shade tried to keep his face from tightening. "Great." He'd tried to pick something that Goth wouldn't be interested in, and Shade knew he despised ice, thought it was some kind of personal insult. Goth must know.

Numb with dread, he led the way down the stone tunnel.

"It's over here," said Shade outside. At least if he led them away from the roost, he'd have more time before Throbb found them. Time to maybe make an escape, lose Goth in the undergrowth. And sunrise not more than twenty minutes away.

"Do you hear that?" Goth asked.

"Yeah," said Marina. "Sounds like a horde of insects."

It was getting louder now, but it had a regularity that made Shade think it wasn't insects at all, but some kind of Human machine. Whatever it was, it was coming their way.

"There's Throbb," said Goth.

Shade looked. Throbb was beating his way toward them, fast. He'd be there in less than a minute.

"What is that?" Marina gasped.

Bearing down on Throbb was some kind of Human flying machine, wings a blur, lights blazing. Throbb started to bellow, but the machine flew over him, drowning out his voice. Shade stared in horror as it came straight for him, and reared overhead. Wind exploded around him.

A dart whistled through the air, grazing his tail, and slammed into a branch. A second dart plunged into Goth's chest. Roaring in anger, the giant bat spiraled down, thrashing as he tried to wrench it free.

"Let's go!" Shade shouted to Marina.

They veered away from the flying machine, hurtling back down into the forest. Shade flew low to the ground, even though he knew it was dangerous. Raccoons, wild dogs, even snakes, could leap up and snap at them. Owls waiting in branches could drop on them like forked lightning. But above the tree line, they'd be easy prey for the Humans, and their deadly darts.

Birds were starting to rise from their nests, and a dawn chorus cut into the icy morning air.

"Where?" he asked Marina urgently. She was the expert.

To his alarm she landed on the ground.

"What're you doing?"

At the base of an elm was a thick bed of rain-matted leaves. Marina quickly nosed around in them, and then started burrowing with her claws and head, pushing her way deeper into the mulch. Shade understood, and instantly followed her lead. Working quickly, they soon hollowed out a deep nest. Scuttling back up to the opening, Marina dragged some leaves across, covering their tracks.

Inside it was damp and cold, and they huddled close together. Shade was so tired his whole body was shaking.

"What happened?" she asked him.

"I saw Throbb eating a bat."

"You're sure?"

He nodded, teeth chattering. "I think the Humans killed Goth. Those darts." He remembered the one that had narrowly missed him, and shivered.

"What about Throbb?"

He shook his head. "When that machine came, I lost sight of him." The image of the limp Brightwing in Throbb's jaws shimmered in his mind again, and he winced. "I hope they got him," he said vengefully.

"I had a feeling about them, you know," she said.

Shade said nothing.

"A couple of nights ago, I woke up in the roost, and Throbb was staring at me, and there was just something about his eyes, hungry. Like I was food."

"Why didn't you tell me?"

"What would you've done?"

He sighed, ashamed. "Laughed. Said you were seeing things. I'm stupid."

Bats who fed on their own kind. They were monsters. No animal he'd ever heard of, not even the owls, did such a thing.

He felt a sudden rush of self-loathing. He'd trusted Goth, believed every word he'd said. Go to the jungle, raise an army, defeat the birds and the beasts once and for all. He'd thought they were going to be allies. He'd thought it was all part of the Promise.

"You wanted to be like them," Marina said.

He nodded miserably. Look at me! he shouted inwardly. Look at how small I am! Who wouldn't want power like that, the power to kill an owl? The power to stop them from burning your roost down, to help your colony and find your father . . .

"But why didn't they just eat us right away?" he asked.

"They needed us at first—to give them directions. After we showed them how to read stars, they didn't need us anymore."

"I thought it was you, Marina. When I first saw him eating that bat, I thought it was you."

"Must have caught a straggler," she said in a dull voice.

He shivered again, and they shuffled closer, enfolding each other in their wings.

"They wanted to kill all of us, the Humans, didn't they," Marina muttered darkly. "My colony was right all along. Humans are evil."

Shade clenched his teeth, not knowing what to say.

"That machine came straight at us," Marina went on. "They knew where we were."

"How?"

"The bands," she breathed. "It must be. They tell them where we are."

Shade's fur bristled. The idea of that machine coming back, those darts plunging into him.

"The bands don't mean anything, do they?" Marina said savagely. "All it does is mark me, so they can come kill us. No wonder my colony drove me off. They were right. I am cursed."

"Don't," Shade said hoarsely.

"And you were right too. The Humans aren't going

to help us. And as long as I'm with you, you're in danger too."

He squeezed his eyes shut, wishing he could drive all thoughts from his head. Everything had collapsed. He didn't know what he had left to believe in. He'd felt so sure when he'd left the echo chamber at Tree Haven. And now, what did he know? The bands meant nothing. What had his father risked his life for? What did Frieda know? Maybe there was no Promise at all. It was a story, a lie, and Bathsheba was right all along. There was only night and day and the law, and that's all there ever would be.

"We're going to find my colony," Shade said grimly. "And we're going to find the truth about the bands. About everything."

Goth fell, the dart deep in his side, limp wings knocking frozen leaves. He hit the ground in a heap. His vision swam, and it was an effort to lift his head. One last try. Drunkenly twisting his neck, he clenched the base of the dart in his teeth and jerked back. The dart ripped clean and blood flowed from the wound. His flanks heaved for air. Some kind of poison in the dart, like those needles they used to stick in him. Fight it, fight it. He was so tired, so heavy.

Blackness, then—

Dry leaves crackling, the ground vibrating, and a pair of gloved hands picked him up. He kept his eyes closed, but he was suddenly, totally awake. He concentrated on the hands, gauged the strength of the fingers, where the grip was weakest. He opened one eye just a slit, and saw the Man from the artificial jungle looking down at him, his face protected behind a plastic hood.

Goth closed his eye, took a long slow breath, and then struck.

He flared his wings, knocking the Man in the face, and making him stumble back with a long, slow moan of surprise. The Man's grip loosened, and Goth wrenched his body free, launching himself into the air. He plunged at the hood, sinking his claws into the fabric and ripping it up and off the Human's head.

The Man was reaching for something at his side, lifting it, trying to aim. Goth darted down, claws lowered, and raked him across the face. The Man dropped the object in his hands, and clutched the gash in his cheek.

"Zotz curse you!" Goth shrieked as he lifted himself up through a gap in the trees, high into the sky. In a nearby field he caught a glimpse of the flying machine, resting on the ground, and two more Humans running into the woods toward the Man.

"Shade!" he cried. "Marina! Throbb!"

"Here! I'm here!"

Flapping toward him was Throbb, and Goth was almost glad to see him.

"I thought they'd killed you!" cried Throbb.

"It was another sleeping potion. Keep flying, this way, we'll get away from them. Where are the other two?"

Throbb's eyes flickered guiltily.

"Throbb?"

"I don't know."

"Why didn't you kill Marina like I told you?"

"I thought I did . . ." Throbb faltered. "It was a Brightwing, all alone, and I killed it, and then I realized it wasn't her. And . . ." He trailed off miserably.

"And what, Throbb?"

"And the runty one saw."

"You idiot," said Goth with quiet loathing. "No wonder he was acting so strangely. I thought they were trying to escape." He looked contemptuously at Throbb. "You let them get away."

"There were darts everywhere, I couldn't see—"

"Shut up."

"But we don't need them," said Throbb. "We can find our own way south now. We'll get back to the jungle faster without the little bats to slow us down."

"We needed the runt. For my plans."

Goth fell silent, furious. He should have done it himself. Killed Marina, made it look like an owl had struck her. Then he would've had Shade safely all to himself.

Now it was ruined. Shade knew they were bat-eaters. How could he possibly win back his trust? But he wouldn't turn back now. He wouldn't be defeated by these little bats. He'd made his promise with Zotz. And so help him, Zotz, he would not fail.

"We're going to follow them," he told Throbb. "We're going to find them."

# PART THREE

# WINTER

It snowed.

At first the flakes came down soft and slow, and Shade weaved his way around them, fascinated by their intricate patterns. He remembered the first time he'd been caught in the rain, and tried to fly between the drops until he was dizzy and exhausted, and very wet anyway. Now he looked up into the sky and was dazzled by the sight, as if the stars were gently falling.

"You can drink them," Marina said. "Watch."

He began catching the snowflakes in his mouth too, letting them melt on his tongue, drinking in midair. He laughed in delight, and the sound startled him. It was two nights since they'd left Goth and Throbb, and they'd flown steadily, keeping the same course, and not talking much. Tonight was warmer than the last, and there was a rising mist. For an hour or so he and Marina played in the snow, laughing and rolling through the silver sky. Trying to forget.

But a wind soon whipped up, driving the snow at a vicious angle so it stung his ears and wings. The stars had been completely blocked out long ago, and it was impossible for them to keep their course.

"We'd better land," Marina said. "We can't see where we're going."

When, the next night, he poked his head out from their roost in a high birch, the whole world had been transformed. He was startled by how bright it was. Glowing in the moonlight, the snow blanketed the earth in gentle swells, forming hills around the bases of trees, and cloaking the branches so they looked soft and fat.

The landscape glittered fiercely. Even a second out of the roost he could feel the warmth being sucked through his fur.

"Have you felt cold like this before?" he asked, teeth chattering.

"Flying's the only way to warm up."

There were no smells. It was as if they were frozen too, or maybe it was just the inside of his nose that was frozen. When he wrinkled it up, his nostrils took a few seconds to sink back into place. And it was so quiet. No insect drone. No frog's croak or cricket's thrum. Panic seized him. Of course the cold would kill and drive away the insects. Where did they go anyway? Did they migrate too?

"What're we going to eat?"

"It's okay, there's still food."

She showed him. Flying low around the base of the elm, she said, "See that?"

He thought it was merely specks of dirt in the smooth snow, until he saw some move—leap, more like it.

"Snow fleas," Marina explained. There were lots of them, and he and Marina moved from tree to tree, snapping them up.

"They're not bad," Shade said. "Better than mosquitoes."

In an open field she showed him a sac of praying mantis eggs hanging from a twig, which poked up through the snow. And in the spindly branches of a maple, a moth cocoon, coated in silver frost. On a dead tree she showed him where the bark had been eaten away by engraver beetles and carpenter ants, and the insects were still there, you only had to scratch and dig down a bit.

It wasn't long before he had a full, warm stomach, and he felt much better.

"You're amazing," he said with admiration.

She laughed. "It's just your first winter. You didn't know."

"How'd you learn all this stuff?"

She looked away. "My parents taught me."

He was sorry he'd reminded her.

"Your mother would've taught you too," she added. "It's no big deal."

"Well, thanks for showing me," he said.

"Sure."

He looked up into the sky and picked out their guiding star. It seemed brighter than ever, as did the others, cold, hard flares of light in the blackness. They flew on through the silver night.

He thought about his father more than ever now, and sometimes, when he didn't think he could fly another minute, he'd force himself into a hypnotic rhythm, where every beat of his wings was one beat closer to finding him: there, and there, and there. Before, it had given him comfort to think he might be with the Humans; now that was almost as horrible as imagining him with owls.

"What is that?" Marina said suddenly. In the distance he picked out dark shapes draped over the bright tree-tops. He drew closer and his throat tightened.

Bat wings. Wings no longer attached to bodies. They were snagged on spiky branches, littered across the white snow. He started to count and gave up when he hit sixty. He could tell by the fringes of fur they were Graywings.

"Owls," said Marina. "Must've been lots of them."

She pointed out their pellets in the snow. Shade couldn't bring himself to look closer. He knew what he would see there. He circled, staring as if hypnotized. They must have been migrating, and the owls had come and attacked, and who knows how many they killed. And then they'd eaten them right here, tearing off the wings first, because there wasn't enough meat on them. He'd seen Goth and Throbb do the same to birds.

"They probably didn't know anything," he said, choking out the words. "Nothing about the closed skies, and the owls just came along and . . . slaughtered them."

"I hate Goth and Throbb," Marina said savagely. "This is their fault too. If they hadn't killed those two lousy pigeons in the city, this wouldn't have happened."

He'd been afraid of this all along. But he'd lied to himself anyway, telling himself that all the bats would fly on ahead of the owl's command to close the skies. They'd escape, for the winter anyway, sleeping safe inside their roosts. But not these Graywings. And who knew how far the owl messengers had gone now.

Maybe even to his own colony.

He ground his jaws together. "I wish I were like Goth. I'd kill them all, I really would. I'd just kill them . . ."

Marina flew in close, nudging against him gently.

"We should get out of here. They might come back."

"I want them to come back," he raged. "I want to get one, just one of them . . ." And he was suddenly sobbing, and all his words flooded together. He held his breath, clenching his whole body until it stopped shaking. He took a ragged breath. He wished she hadn't seen him cry.

"I'm sorry."

She shook her head. "For what?" And he saw that her eyes were bright with tears too. "But we really should go."

After flying an hour, she asked him, "Do you think they're alive, Goth and Throbb?"

"You saw that dart hit him."

"It's just . . . they know which way we're going."

The thought had never left the back of Shade's mind—that they might be alive, and that they could follow Shade's star.

"Even if they're alive, they might have given up and gone due south."

Marina nodded eagerly. "They're not built for the cold. Remember how they shivered all the time? I don't think their fur's as thick as ours. They don't need it in the jungle." She paused. "You think we should change course, just in case?"

"I'd like to," he said. "But we'd just get lost."

"What's the next landmark?" she asked. "You didn't tell them that too, did you?" There was a hint of reproach in her voice.

"No," he said, offended. "Sound maps are the secret of the colony."

"Yeah, yeah. So what is it?"

Shade shut his eyes and tried to calm his tired mind. He watched:

The night world, scrolling out to the horizon.

The land slowly rising, the trees frozen in ice. Rock heaving up into the sky, white peaks.

"We go higher," he said to Marina. "The land reaches way up."

"Mountains," she said grimly.

"There's more . . ."

The baying of a wolf.

Then, from nowhere, something massive loomed up from the darkness, and all Shade could see was the beast's two pointed ears, surging toward him.

"Wolves," he said with a jolt.

"What d'you mean?" she asked impatiently.

"There's the sound of wolves." It didn't make sense. Why would his mother tell him to seek out wolves? They were the most feared beasts in the north.

"We're supposed to go where the wolves are." He shook his head. "And it's like we're supposed to go close, because I see one wolf, all white, jumping at me, and the last thing I see is his pointed ears."

"That's the landmark, huh?" Marina said.

"I'm sorry—"

"It's next to useless," she snapped. "It doesn't mean

anything, unless your mother wanted you to get eaten."

"It's what she sang me," he said firmly.

She sighed. "Okay, okay. At least we know we're headed for mountains. We've just got to keep going and hope you recognize the right place. At least if Goth and Throbb are alive, they won't last long up there." She looked at him. "But neither will we."

"There's something wrong with my wing," Throbb said. He folded it in, pushed it out. "It's gone hard near the tip."

Goth yawned. "It's because you're a miserable weakling," he said. He wasn't about to tell Throbb about the stiffness of his own wings. How every night he had to limber up before taking flight. Curse this cold. There was no getting away from it. It seeped through his skin and settled deep in his bones.

"It doesn't look right," Throbb whined, still staring at his wing.

Goth looked and saw that the membrane was slightly mottled, like a blister. In the jungle, he'd seen wings rot and fall off, but never anything like these raised sores.

"I don't see anything," he grunted. But he quickly checked his own wing tips. They were fine. Throbb was weak, that's why his wings were blistering.

How long did the winter last? Four months, isn't that what Shade had said? He knew they wouldn't survive out in the open for much longer. They'd have to find a warm place. They'd have to reach Hibernaculum.

Food was harder to come by. The land was frozen. All Goth had managed to find in the past two nights was a squirrel, which he'd rooted out of its hollow in a tree. His eyes strayed to Throbb. He'd lost weight since they'd left the false jungle, but there was still plenty of meat on him. Saliva gushed into his mouth.

"What?" Throbb asked nervously.

"Nothing," said Goth. Throbb might still be useful to him.

Zotz would not let him freeze. He was being tested, and only his cowardice would be punished. Every night they set course by the star Shade had shown him. It was only a matter of time before they overtook him. Tomorrow night they'd catch up, he was sure of it.

Then he'd get the rest of the sound map from Shade.

And then he'd eat him.

He would arrive at Hibernaculum with the sad news of Shade's death, and befriend the Silverwings.

He would have a warm place to get him through the rest of the winter.

And all the food he needed.

# TRANSFORMATION

Shade was almost always cold now. He tried to remember Tree Haven on a hot summer night, and couldn't.

The ground had been rising steadily for the past three hours. In the distance rose bony mountains, with gaunt icy summits.

"I don't like it," said Marina. "Why would your colony go this way? It's so cold."

Shade stared miserably at the landscape. There were fewer trees and shrubs now, and the ground was rockier. A roost would be hard to find. There were certainly wolves around too. He could hear them now, sending up their mournful and terrifying howls.

Without warning a gale came screaming down from the mountain, and suddenly the world was a white swirl.

"Marina!" he shouted above the noise. "Where are you?"

"Here, here!" she said, and he could see her shadow as she struggled to pull alongside him.

Eddies of snow drove into his eyes. His echo vision was nothing but a painful silver haze. He desperately shook his wings, heavy with snow, but it was no use.

"I can't stay up!"

"We'll land."

But where? he wondered anxiously as they veered

clumsily to the ground. It was all snow and ice—and wolves. Searching desperately for a good tree, he caught sight of a snowy ridge jutting out from the hillside.

"There, over there!" he shouted, angling his wings. There was no time to make a pass and check for birds. He stretched out his claws and landed up to his chin in snow. Shivering, he lifted his head clear and scrambled over to Marina.

"I thought maybe there'd be a cave," he said.

"It's not rock," Marina told him, tapping with her claws. "It's wood. It's a roof."

In surprise Shade peered over the edge, and could now make out wooden walls, caked with snow.

"There's no light coming from the windows," he said. "You think there's anyone inside?"

From somewhere on the mountainside rose the long howl of a wolf.

"We'll have to take our chances," said Marina. "It's too late to find anywhere else. Dig."

Together they shoveled down through the snow until they found a warped wooden plank with a gap big enough for them to squeeze through. Inside, Shade gratefully shook the snow from his fur. It was a large dark space under the rafters, surprisingly warm, and filled with boxes, piles of old blankets, and other Human objects he didn't recognize. A tiny window set in one wall let in a pale swirling light. Outside the wind moaned.

He wondered if his mother and the rest of his colony were trapped in the same storm, or whether they'd moved beyond it, and were just leaving them farther and farther behind. He sighed. There was nothing he could do about it.

His fur suddenly tingled, and he looked at Marina. She was holding herself stiff, her chest barely moving.

They weren't alone. With his eyes he found the exit crack in the roof, ready to fly at any moment. There was a leathery creak of wings, the scratch of a claw gripping wood.

"One of us," came a faint whisper, ". . . one of us . . ."

Shade's flesh crawled. He tensed, ready to spring for the exit. He'd rather take his chances in the storm than face some whispering ghoul . . .

"Wait," Marina hissed to him.

The creak of wings was all around them now, and then another voice, near the ceiling—

"Yes, she's one of us."

And another at the far end of the loft—

"You're right, she's one of us!"

"Who's there!" Shade demanded.

All at once, a hundred bats were in the air, fluttering up from their hiding places under the rafters and along the walls. He'd never seen so many different types. He spotted Graywings, a few Silverwings, but mostly they were completely new to him. Bats with black faces and small, mouse-shaped noses; pale bats with enormous ears that seemed in danger of toppling over; bats with flamboyant crests of fur; bats with huge snouts, dappled fur, small sad eyes.

They must have come from a dozen different colonies. But they had one thing in common.

They were all banded.

A female with bright fur settled beside Marina.

"Another Brightwing," the bat said happily. "I'm Penelope."

"Penelope," Marina murmured, staring in amazement. "I heard about you. But they said you'd been banded and it killed you. Three years ago."

Penelope shook her head, smiling. "No. They made that up. They just expelled me from the colony, because they were superstitious. There're dozens of us here, and the bands haven't hurt anyone."

Marina nodded, and Shade could see her eyes fill with tears. She cleared her throat. "You're the first Brightwing I've seen in a while."

"We're so glad you came. It's amazing you could find us in this storm."

"Just luck."

"No," Penelope said, "the band drew you to us. That's how we all found our way. We're connected. That's one of the reasons the Humans gave them to us. So we could all gather together—"

My father. The thought leaped into Shade's head. Was this where his father had come? To be with all the other banded bats?

"Is there a Cassiel here?" he asked urgently. "A Silverwing?"

Just by the blank look on Penelope's face, Shade knew the answer, and he felt himself sag with disappointment.

"There's no one here by that name," came another voice. Fluttering over to them was an older male with the longest ears Shade had ever seen. They shot high up in the air, making his face look small by comparison. His echo vision must be incredible, Shade thought. He wondered if this bat could see into the past and future like Zephyr.

"I'm Scirocco," said the bat, roosting beside them. "Welcome."

Shade couldn't help noticing that this greeting was directed mainly at Marina, and Scirocco gave him only the quickest of nods. He looked intently at Marina's band.

"Yes, by the shape and markings I'd guess not a full year has passed since you received the band. Am I right?"

She nodded. "I got it last spring."

"And do you know the importance of it? Do you know it's part of Nocturna's Promise?"

Shade looked at Marina, and her eyes fell away sadly. She said nothing.

"What's the matter?" Penelope asked.

"I used to think that," she said softly. "That it meant something. But it's not true."

"Why do you say that?"

"We met other banded bats, not from here, but from the jungle. They were big, much bigger than us. They could kill birds, even owls. And they ate bats."

Penelope looked aghast, and a murmur of horror passed through the loft.

"Go on," Scirocco urged her gently.

Marina told him everything that had happened since they'd met Goth and Throbb. The long-eared bat listened attentively as she spoke, occasionally interrupting with questions. After she'd told him about the flying machine that had come, and the Humans who had tried to kill them with darts, he nodded.

"The Humans imprisoned those bats for a reason."

"Goth said they were studying them," Shade offered. He was starting to feel left out. He had a part in this story too, and he didn't like it that Marina got to tell everything. But Scirocco only looked at him briefly before turning back to her.

"That's what they told you, but you know they're liars. The Humans knew what a danger they'd be to the rest of us. They wanted to keep those bats locked out of the skies. They weren't meant to escape."

"No," said Marina. "But why were they banded, then?"

The same question had been on the tip of Shade's tongue, but she beat him to it.

"You said their bands were black. I was struck by that detail. Not a single bat here has been banded in black. Our bands are bright silver, like the sun, because we are meant to return to the sun. Any bat who wears black can never leave the night. Those bats have been marked, certainly, but not as part of Nocturna's Promise."

Marina looked quickly at Shade, and he could see the spark of hope in her eyes. What Scirocco said did seem reasonable. But there were still a few things that didn't make sense. He cleared his throat.

"But why did the Humans try to kill us?" he asked quietly. "One of their darts nearly hit me."

Again, Scirocco gave him the quickest of glances. It was just like being back at Tree Haven again, and Chinook ignoring him, and nobody listening. He felt unpleasantly small. He had no band. He was an outsider here, and it rankled him. He'd seen the echo chamber, he'd been told by Frieda he had a brightness. He was searching for the answers too.

"I don't think the Humans had any intention of harming you," Scirocco replied. "They shot Goth, yes, and we can only hope they also shot Throbb. They weren't hunting you. They were protecting you."

Shade let out his breath slowly. Could it be true?

Marina nodded slowly. "We were stupid to fly away. They might have helped us."

"Don't worry," said Scirocco. "Nocturna's Promise is about to come true. We will return to the light of day. And we will become Human."

Human.

Shade listened, dumbfounded. Never in his life would he have guessed. Whenever he'd thought of Nocturna's Promise, he'd always assumed they would return to the light of day as bats. But Scirocco said there would be a transformation first, and all those who had been banded would become Human. That's how they would finally win back the sun. They'd never have to live in fear of the birds and beasts again.

He watched Marina as she listened. Since leaving Goth and Throbb, she'd been gloomy, locked inside her own thoughts, but now her face shone with excitement, and when she caught his eye, she gave him a brilliant smile.

He had to look away. Why wasn't he happier? He'd come to find out the secret of the bands, and now he had it. What Scirocco said had the ring of truth. So why did it bother him? Maybe it was just shock, this new idea of leaving one body for another. Human. How he'd envied them in the cathedral. He'd wanted their strength, their size, but did he want to *become* one of them? They seemed slow, heavy. They couldn't see at night.

They couldn't fly.

Shade summoned up his courage. He felt like he was back before the elders in the upper roost at Tree Haven.

"How do you know for sure—about the transformation, I mean."

"Because it's already started," Scirocco replied.

"Human . . . Human . . ." came an excited whisper from the rafters.

"Watch," Scirocco said.

He moved to a clear space in the middle of the wooden floor. "It's coming soon. I can feel it in my bones," he said, closing his eyes, his brow wrinkling with concentration. "My bat bones will soon become human bones. My legs will stretch and grow long and become Human legs . . ."

With a quick thrust of his wrists, the long-eared bat jerked upright onto his hind legs, swaying slightly for only a moment before achieving balance. His tail dragged the ground.

"Transform!" the bats overhead chanted. "Transform!"

Ponderously, Scirocco took a few steps forward on his hind legs, wings folded tight against his sides, head thrust forward. Walking, like a Human.

A weird energy was filling up the loft, and Shade looked at Marina in alarm. She was staring at Scirocco, amazed, her eyes blazing.

"My claws will be blunted, my fingers shrink!" Scirocco was saying. "My fur will thin, my face will smooth and flatten. My wings will wither and fall from my shoulders like a snake's useless skin!"

"Transform! Transform!"

Shade swallowed, his heart racing. Scirocco's steps were more confident now, and his wings were folded in so tight they seemed to have disappeared . . . and his face looked paler, less furry . . .

Shade's echo vision wavered. The very air in the loft seemed charged with light and sound. He shook his head, gazing in wonder at Scirocco. What was happening?

"I'm telling you all now," Scirocco cried out, "that I will grow tall and strong and powerful and walk into the light as a Human!"

"Transform!"

Scirocco's body shuddered and suddenly burst its own skin, towering up into the air.

"Transform!" wailed the bats in a fever, and when Shade glanced at Marina, he saw that she was chanting too. He felt intensely alone, and afraid. He whirled back to Scirocco, and cried out in alarm.

Standing in the middle of the loft was a Human. But he still had bat eyes, and pointed ears jutted out from his head. And when he smiled, the teeth were still bat's teeth, with sharp fangs plunging down from the upper jaw.

"Human! Human!"

Shade clamped shut his eyes, overcome. There was something not right about it, something unnatural. When he looked again, the Human had disappeared. Scirocco was back on the ground, a large-eared bat with pale fur on four legs. The others in the loft had fallen into an exhausted silence. All he could hear was the sound of their panting.

"You see," said Scirocco triumphantly. "We are very close. It won't be long before the Humans come for us, and Nocturna lets us be fully transformed forever!"

Scirocco looked kindly at Marina.

"Join us," he said. "Wait with us for the coming of the light. It won't be long."

"Stay," said the other Brightwing, Penelope. "Please stay."

And a chorus went up from the other bats too. "Stay, stay!"

Marina looked at him. "Why don't we, Shade?"

"No," said Scirocco sternly. "The Silverwing can't stay."

"Why not?" demanded Marina.

But Shade had been expecting this.

"He's not one of the chosen," Scirocco said. "Nocturna would be angry if we let the unworthy stay. She might decide to hold all of us back from the transformation. Without a band, there is no promise."

"My father was banded," Shade said indignantly, "and the elder of—"

"That's no concern of ours," said the long-eared bat. "Those who are not banded will never become Human. They will die in the dark, with all the others who haven't been chosen." Scirocco turned and looked Shade full in the eyes for the first time. "I'm sorry, but that is the truth."

Shade turned away, humiliated and angry. He'd come all this way, searching for an answer, and now he'd found it. But he was no part of it. Chosen. How did you get to be chosen? What had he done wrong? If Marina could be banded, why couldn't he? She wasn't so special. If she had one, *he* should have one. All his life he'd been on the fringes of things, the runt. And now this. He felt his face harden. Out of the corner of his eye, he could see Marina watching him anxiously.

"You stay," he told her in a tight voice.

She shook her head, and the pain in her eyes made him melt. He turned to her. She'd waited so long, alone for most of it, hoping there was something special about her band. And now she'd found the answer, and a group of bats who, finally, didn't drive her away but wanted her to stay with them forever.

"You've got to," he said. "You've got to stay."

"But—"

"I'm going to find my colony. My father."

Her eyes flickered, and she scratched her claws unhappily against the wood. "It's not that far, right? You're probably almost there." She looked at him desperately. "You'll be all right, won't you?"

She wanted him to say yes, he could tell. He nodded vigorously.

"Oh, sure, I know the rest of the way. I've got the map. You helped me a lot."

He looked at the small window high in the wall, and by the light he could tell the snow wasn't blowing anymore. He couldn't even hear the wind. There were still about three hours of the night left.

"I should get going."

She came close to him and wrapped her wings around him tightly. She was so warm.

"I'm sorry," she whispered in his ear. "You understand, don't you?"

He nodded, and coughed impatiently, driving away his tears.

"Good luck, Shade."

"You too," he said. He hurried to the crack in the roof and flung himself into the night without looking back.


Goth angled a nearly frozen wing and circled over the barren terrain. Ice matted his snout. But his eyes blazed. He peered intently at the ground.

"What is it?" Throbb asked.

Goth sniffed, then lifted a claw to knock the ice from his flared nostrils. He sniffed again, straining for every faint odor in the frozen air.

He smiled. Zotz had provided for him once again.

He jerked his head down at a Human cabin, half covered by snow, and nearly invisible against the mountain.

"Food," he said. "And lots of it."

# WOLF EARS

Never had Shade felt so lonely. He'd got so used to Marina's company that it seemed impossible she wasn't at his wing tip, or just ahead, scolding him to hurry up.

The whole world was a vast, aching echo—the mangy trees, the rocks, all hollow, all joyless.

Scirocco's words rang in his mind: You will die in the dark, with all the others who haven't been chosen. He had no place in the future. Nocturna's Promise was not for him; he would never live to walk into the light of day as a Human.

But Marina would. And Frieda. His father too. It was fine for them. Anger swept through him. Why hadn't Frieda told him? Did she really not know, or was she just keeping it from him, because he didn't have one of those precious bands? And what about his father? Why wasn't he here to help, to explain things to him? Probably just hiding away with his band somewhere, waiting to become Human. Shade shook his head. And what would happen to him? And his mother, and all the other unbanded bats?

He didn't want to believe it.

He stared up at the stars, and watched as they flickered, as if they really were on the shimmering underside of Nocturna's giant wings. All the bat goddess had to do was close her wings and the whole night would disappear, replaced by day. Open them again, and the stars would return.

What was she doing up there, Shade wondered, if she was even there at all? What did she have in mind for him, one runt of a bat, trying to find his own colony?

The stars weren't telling.

They were always silent. They had no song, none that he could pick up anyway. Maybe Zephyr could hear them, but Shade knew his hearing would never be that good.

Ahead, the mountain peaks soared. How could he ever fly high enough to get over them? He sniffed, looking to the east and west to gauge the time of night. An hour, maybe a little more. There was no way he'd make it over tonight. He wanted to lose himself in the whistle of wind against his ears.

For the first time he felt afraid in the night. He was seeing sound shadows, smudges of silvery movement at the edge of his echo vision. A clump of dead leaves whirled in the air, and became Goth, spreading his wings toward him. An owl's distant cry resolved itself into a ghoulish rendition of his own name: "Shade! Shade!"

He was suddenly struck by the vastness of the night, all the empty space yawning around him. Maybe there *was* something terrible about the darkness, and he'd just never noticed before now.

There was something behind him.

Hackles rising, he looked back just as something sailed over him, so low it brushed his wings. And there she was ahead of him, her bright fur shimmering in the starlight, like something from a dream.

"What're you doing?" he demanded.

"Hey, you don't sound too happy to see me!"

"You . . . you scared me!"

"I'm coming with you."

"But—why'd you change your mind?"

She circled back and drew alongside. "It just didn't feel right, staying there without you."

"I'd have been fine on mine own," he said, trying to look annoyed, and not having much success.

"Oh, I know," she said quickly. "But I said I'd find your colony with you, and it just feels like quitting if I don't see it through."

Shade didn't know what to say. He was so grateful to have her back. But it made him sad to think she was passing up this chance for happiness.

"Are you sure?" he said carefully.

She hesitated for only a second, then nodded. "The only reason they were nice to me was this thing on my forearm. It didn't have anything to do with me. They were just like those Graywings we met, remember? They liked you, and hated me because of the band. And these other bats weren't any different. Liked me, hated you because you *didn't* have a band. It's just a piece of metal, after all."

He looked at her, surprised. "You don't believe them, then?"

She sighed. "Part of me wants to—more than anything. It sounds so wonderful. And the way Scirocco started to change like that. . . . You think it was a trick?"

"I thought about it. Like a sound picture he was singing into all our heads. Or maybe it was everyone else in the loft singing it, just hoping for it so much . . . what do I know?"

"I kept thinking of something Zephyr told us. Remember, he said beware of metal on wings. Maybe this is what he meant—all these bats with bands. Because my heart tells me it can't be true. And . . . the idea of turning into a Human, I don't know if I like that."

"Me neither," said Shade enthusiastically. "Think of all the things we couldn't do. I'm pretty happy being a bat."

"I know. Anyway, the whole thing just doesn't seem fair. I didn't do anything to earn that band. I mean, why'd I get a band and not someone else? Not you?"

"Exactly," he said. "I should have one of those things too."

"Well, I don't know about that," she said, and then smiled mischievously. "I mean, you're not quite as fabulous as me, are you?"

He laughed. "No, I'm sure not," he said gratefully.

Marina looked thoughtful again. "Anyway, if what they say is true, I can always go back. After we've found your colony, and your father. But as far as I'm concerned, you're the only bat who's liked me because of who I am. You didn't care one way or another about the band. That makes you the best friend I've ever had."

They slept that day huddled close, under the frozen roots of a lone pine on the mountainside.

The howling of wolves filled the air.

They were nearly at the summit, and it was slow going. The wind was against them, making every wingbeat an effort. Shade looked down and picked out a she-wolf and her mate, loping across the snow, going higher into the mountains.

"Must be a lair somewhere up here," he said grimly. His mother wouldn't be leading him into a wolves' lair, would she? He dragged up the sound map again and again, studying the images his mother had sung to him. But he was no wiser. "We'll just have to keep going."

A faint whistling made him look back over his wing and do a quick sonic sweep. The sound dissolved in the air, and he picked out nothing. It wasn't the first time tonight he'd heard the weird metallic whistle. Just the wind, he supposed, screaming through whippy branches.

His bones ached, the leather of his wings creaked with cold. He doggedly pounded the frigid air, up, down, up, down. The wind burned his ears, and his sound sight was dulled as a result, all his echo images blurred and sluggish. He knew they'd freeze to death if they didn't make it over the summit tonight. They had no food in their stomachs, not even a single snow flea. How sweet it would be to just wrap himself up in his wings and drift and drift, down, down, down . . .

"Wake up!" Marina shouted into his ear, and he came to his senses with a horrible jolt. He'd almost fallen asleep, and was keeling over to one side.

"Thanks," he mumbled, righting himself.

"Don't do that to me," said Marina, clearly shaken. "Stay awake. Talk to me, sing, I don't care, just don't doze off."

Shade shook his head, forcing himself to take a deep breath of the icy air. It burned his lungs, but at least woke him up.

They skimmed over a jagged peak and the wind unleashed its full fury.

They were at the very top of the world.

Stretching out on either side was a range of ice-clad mountains. His eyes watered madly and he narrowed them to mere slits. For a moment the howling of wolves rose above the gale, and he saw not two but dozens, gathered before the entrance of a cave on one of the steep slopes. He looked at Marina.

"I'm not going down there!" she shouted.

"What else can we do?"

"It's suicide!"

"She sang me wolves!"

"Wolf ears," said Marina, and suddenly she was laughing.

She's gone crazy, Shade thought. She's finally cracked up with the cold and exhaustion. She was babbling and laughing at the same time, maybe imagining a giant white wolf in midair, bounding toward them. Maybe she was right, he'd believe just about anything now.

"Wolf *ears*!" she shouted at him again, more insistently.

And he looked.

Off to one side were two mountain peaks thrusting into the sky, a deep valley carved out between them. It was just like the image in his mother's sound map, not an animal at all, but a mountain pass, covered in snow and looking for all the world like the ears of a giant white wolf.

"There they are."

Goth hunched his shoulders, riding the gale-force winds that swept over the mountaintops. Up ahead he could see Shade and Marina, angling for a valley between two icy peaks. He'd been following them for the past hour, steadily gaining on them up the slope.

He hung back, not wanting to be seen just yet. When he struck, there would be no mistakes. Despite the blood-freezing cold, he felt strong. Last night he'd feasted as he hadn't feasted since his days in the jungle. He glanced with satisfaction at the bands of glittering metal that festooned his forearms. They were smaller than his own band, easier to bend, and he'd ripped them from his prey, sometimes snapping wristbones to get them. His new hunting trophies.

Beside him, Throbb pounded along. The blister on his wing tip had spread, and looked angrier than before. Throbb said it burned with cold. Weakling. Goth was disgusted by him. But right now, his stomach was full, and Throbb did not seem so appetizing. Later, perhaps. He fastened his eyes and ears on Shade and Marina.

A blast of wind surged beneath him, whirling through his metal bands and sending a brief but piercing whistle across the mountaintops.

# RAT

Shade heard the eerie whistle in a lull of the wind's roar.

He turned and saw them, hanging in the sky like an image torn from a nightmare. For some reason he felt almost no surprise. He'd thought about this moment so much, played it out over and over in his head, that it seemed merely inevitable. But that noise . . . what was that terrible whistling noise?

"Marina," he croaked, "they're here."

"What?" She whipped her head around, staring. "No, they should be dead . . ."

A vicious crosswind buffeted them both to one side, and they turned their attention back to the wolf ears.

"We can maybe lose them on the other side," he said.

"I'd trim your wings if I were you. This is going to be rough."

Shade swallowed. The twin mountain peaks heaved on the horizon. He had a sudden flash of his mother's sound map—he could understand how he'd first thought the mountain was a wolf, lunging toward him. It looked just like that now, as he was pitched forward.

His wings were stiff with frost. Shunted to the side again, he adjusted his course, aiming for the narrow pass. But he was coming in too close to the left peak, and the wind wouldn't let him bank.

"Shade!" he heard Marina cry out to his right—as if from a great distance.

He saw icy rock hurtling toward him. He was going to crash. He tried to pull up, braking so sharply with his wings, he thought they'd snap like frozen twigs. Everything seemed very slow, the incoming rocks, the wind in his ears. It occurred to him to suck in his belly, draw up his legs and claws. He felt nothing but a distant disappointment that his life was going to end so soon.

He skimmed a hard patch of snow, felt its sharp coldness, and with the gentlest bounce was airborne again, wings beating furiously. He was clear. He veered diagonally back into the sky toward Marina.

"You are so lucky!" he heard her shout above the wind.

They streamed through the wolf ears, and the mountain face dropped away dizzyingly, scooping down to pure darkness. Shade felt his stomach plunge. What was down there? It was too far for him to see with his sound sight. For all he knew the world had ended right here and now.

"It's the only way to go," Marina said.

Shade glanced back over his shoulder and saw Goth and Throbb, riding the wind through the wolf ears, gaining. With their powerful wings, they'd overtake them in a few minutes.

"All right," said Shade grimly.

He stopped flapping and folded his wings in tight. Marina followed his lead. He waited for himself to slow down, the wind carrying him for a few moments before he began to sag. He let his body tilt forward, nose leading, and plunged, down into the starless abyss like a hailstone. His stomach leaped into his throat. He'd always loved flying, the excitement of a steep dive, but this was altogether different. This was faster than he'd ever flown, maybe faster than any bat ever had.

He could barely breathe, the air smashing against his nostrils. The wind stabbed at his eyes like ice pellets, and he shut them tight. Even his mind's eye was nothing but pure blackness, sometimes blossoming into bright star bursts from the wind's howl in his ears. He was still too far from the ground to pick up anything. For the first time in his life he felt blind, and terribly vulnerable. He had no idea where Marina was, no idea if the world even existed anymore. At any moment he felt that his whole shaking body might come apart at the seams. For now he just hoped that Goth and Throbb had lost sight of them and were still circling the mountain peaks.

With every second he could feel the air getting warmer, the ice on his wings pearling into droplets, streaming behind him. And then, a glimmer.

The topmost branches of a tree . . .

Then dozens of treetops, spreading out into a forest . . .

A hill.

Fields on all sides.

He almost cried with relief. The whole world was coming back, painting itself in silver in his head. Carefully, he unfurled just the tips of his wings, and angled them into the wind, starting to slow himself. Then, gradually, he extended more and more, bringing himself gracefully out of his free fall. He opened his eyes and looked out over the rolling landscape. Up ahead were Human lights, but nowhere near as many as the city.

"Marina!" he called out.

"Over here!" Her bright fur stood out against the night.

"Did we lose them?" He gazed back up into the sky, the mountain a vast shadow blotting out the stars.

From high above came a faint whistling noise, quickly building to an ear-splitting shriek.

"No . . ." he muttered in disbelief.

The giant bats plummeted from the heavens, wings fanned out to break their fall. And that noise, that horrible shrieking noise!

"Come on!" Marina shouted at him.

He felt like he was flapping through water, his wings slow and heavy. Marina jerked her head toward the lights.

"If we can make it, we can find somewhere to hide."

There were no high towers here, just rows of low Human buildings, a few machines rolling noisily in between. Behind them came the ghoulish whistling noise. He thought he could smell them, their hot foul breath.

They banked sharply over a broad road, strung with wires and lights, and flanked by bright buildings. Shade looked back and could see Goth's eyes flash in the glare. Throbb was swerving off to one side—he was going to come around, cut them off.

"Down!" Shade shouted to Marina.

He dived toward the street.

"Where are we going?" Marina demanded.

He was too breathless to answer but she stuck by him as they streaked straight down. He had no idea what he was doing. He swerved around a bundle of wires, veered past a skinny metal box filled with circular flashing lights. A machine rolled past, spitting up noise and fumes. The ground was coming up fast and he prepared to pull up sharply, maybe swerve in between two buildings—

When he saw the metal grate at the side of the road. A drizzle of rainwater ran through one of the narrow slits. He measured it with his echo vision in a second. Maybe, just maybe . . .

"Fold your wings!" he shouted.

Without slowing, he dropped headfirst for the grate and at the last moment, pulled his wings tight and plunged beneath the earth.

Deep inside the dripping shaft, Shade peered up at Goth, his jaws fastened around the metal grate, trying to lift it. Throbb sank his claws through one of the slits, and was pulling with all his might. Shade looked worriedly at Marina.

"You think they can move it?" he whispered.

Marina shook her head. "I don't know."

A metal *clunk* answered the question. Shade jolted in alarm. Goth and Throbb had managed to lift the metal grate, just a fraction of an inch, for just a second, before it clanged back down.

"Better find another way out," Marina hissed.

Shade didn't want to go deeper. He'd never liked being underground, all the weight of the earth hanging over his head. But what choice did they have? He fluttered warily down to the bottom of the shaft with Marina. A long tunnel stretched out in two directions.

"I guess it doesn't really matter," said Marina, looking both ways. "There's got to be another shaft that'll lead back up. Right?"

"Yeah, right," said Shade, trying to sound hopeful.

The tunnel was wide enough for them to fly carefully, avoiding the oily sludge seeping along the bottom. It stank down here, of stagnant water, stale air, Human garbage.

"The dart hit him," Shade muttered. "I saw it."

"Maybe he ripped it out in time."

"They have no right being alive."

Up ahead was a glimmering in the roof of the tunnel.

"I think that's it," said Marina hopefully. "There's another shaft."

Shade flew toward the light, was about to veer up into the shaft and—

Teeth. That's what he saw first. Just bared teeth swinging down toward him, snapping. He cried out and recoiled, flapping backward and nearly crashing into Marina.

Two sinewy rats were dangling from the ceiling by their claws, their faces narrowed to fierce slits. There were others now too, swarming along the walls of the shaft, blocking their escape.

"This way!" shouted Marina, flying farther down the tunnel.

"Trespassers!" the rats shouted after them. "We'll get you. You can't get out!"

The rats started tapping their claws loudly on the stone walls, *tap taptap tap taptaptap*, the sound carrying down after Shade and Marina, and past them into the distance. Warning the others, Shade realized in panic.

"There're more," Marina said suddenly. "Up ahead. I can hear them."

Shade cast his sonic gaze down the long tunnel, and the silver image of a dozen rats came back to him, slick-backed creatures scuttling through the sludge, on the walls, on the ceiling. His wingbeats faltered. They'd be cut off if they kept going. But not far from where they were, a small pipe slanted down.

"Here," he said impetuously.

It was too narrow to fly: They could just squeeze through on all fours, one behind the other. Water gushed past his claws. And all the time, through the walls—*tap taptaptap tap tap*. How many rats were down here? All his instincts were against this, going farther underground. He could feel every inch deeper they went, just that much farther from the surface, from the sky.

Behind them came the pounding of many clawed feet.

"Hurry, hurry," he urged Marina over his shoulder.

The pipe opened up ahead, and he scrambled through so quickly he tumbled out the end and plummeted into murky water.

He came up, gasping in panic, thrashing his water-logged wings. Beside him, Marina was scrabbling to keep her head up. They weren't far from the shore, and managed to paddle clumsily over to solid rock, sodden and shivering.

They were in a broad circular tunnel, half filled with deep water, not the sluggish trickle of the higher tunnels, but fast moving. Shade watched it seep past, glinting darkly.

"What now?" Marina said, looking anxiously back up the pipe. "They'll be coming soon."

For a brief moment Shade wished he were Goth. He wished he had huge jaws to bare, giant wings to spread and batter his enemies.

"Come on," he said doggedly, hurrying down the side of the tunnel, clinging to the curved stone wall. Must be a tunnel leading up, must be a way out somewhere . . .

But there was something coming, not an animal, but a thing, riding on the water. Around a bend in the tunnel came a raft, a large, ragged square of wood. On either side, Shade could see rats, swimming alongside, steering it. And riding on the deck were more rats, scanning the water.

"There!" one of them shouted. "Faster!"

Shade turned to face it. It was coming so quickly, and he was too tired to crawl or swim. With Marina at his side, he watched as the raft swiftly overtook them.

High above the town, Goth circled, watching for Shade and Marina.

"They can't stay down there forever," Throbb said.

"When they surface, we'll see them."

He was angry at himself for losing them. He looked at Throbb, considered biting him to make himself feel better. He hoped they would surface, and he'd be in the right place at the right time to spot them.

At the edge of the town he made out vast piles of Human garbage. Even in the frozen air, his sensitive nostrils could pick out the pungent smell of rotting food. Garbage meant rats. Lots of them.

"We'll feed over there," he told Throbb. "And wait them out."

# ROMULUS AND REMUS

The raft glided through the watery maze of underground tunnels. On deck, Shade lay crouched on all fours, shivering beside Marina. There was a rat guard beside each of them, sharp teeth closed lightly around their wings, just in case they tried to break free and fly.

"What're you staring at?" one of the guards growled at Shade.

Shade glanced away. He'd been looking at the rats, struck by how physically similar they were to him. He'd never noticed. Of course, he'd never been this close to rats before. Naturally they were bigger. But if you imagined them with wings . . .

"Bat spies," said the chief guard with loathing.

"We're not spies," said Shade again wearily.

"Tell it to the prince." And the guard laughed unpleasantly, reveling in some secret joke.

Gliding down the waterways, they passed more and more rats on the shores, their eyes flashing in the darkness. Human garbage bobbed in the water. Shade longed to fly away. Beyond the end of the tunnel, he could make out teeming movement: rats, hundreds of them. Farther on was some kind of building. The water was shallower now, and Shade noticed that the rats on the sides of the raft were no longer swimming, but scrabbling along the bottom on all fours.

The tunnel opened out into a much bigger space. High stone walls ran with sludge leaking from dozens of grates. Rats stood hunched at every opening, peering down at them. It seemed every surface was covered with rats. On the ground they writhed in the muck.

The raft ground ashore.

"Move!" the guards barked at Shade and Marina, their jaws tightening on their wings.

Shade walked with difficulty through the mud, the swarm of rats parting to let them pass. The smell of them made him wince, his stomach lurching in disgust. He stumbled. Bats weren't meant to walk on all fours. The crowd jeered. They ground their teeth hungrily, a horrible, bone scraping that set Shade's fur on edge. He looked at Marina, spattered in grime, dragging her claws out of the sucking mud.

They were drawing closer to some kind of rat palace, constructed of garbage: squashed cartons and gnarled plastic and crinkled shiny paper. On a wide platform, high above the mud, slouched the biggest rat of all. His rolls of fat squished out from either side of his corpulent belly. And his teeth, when he showed them, were long and grooved and tarnished with old food.

"They're not kneeling," he said to the guards.

"Kneel before the prince," the chief guard shouted, batting their heads down.

"Do you know who I am?" the fat rat asked.

"The prince?" Marina offered after a pause.

"Guard," said the prince, and the rat beside Marina nipped the edge of her wing. She cried out.

"I won't tolerate insolence in my court," said the prince. He turned to the chief guard. "How did they get inside?"

"The far north grate, Prince Remus."

"And why wasn't it guarded? Who was on duty?"

"Croll, Your Highness."

"Have him dismissed at once."

"He's disappeared, Your Highness."

"I won't tolerate this. Guards must keep to their posts at all times. Do you hear? We've got to be on guard at all times!"

He turned his nervous eyes back to Shade and Marina.

"You're spies, aren't you?"

"No," said Shade.

"Sent to gather information for a surprise attack."

Shade shook his head again.

"How dare you!" bellowed the prince. "How dare you mock me!"

The guard beside Shade ground his teeth threateningly.

"You think because my kingdom lies in the shadow of a mountain, I'm cut off?" His chest heaved with anger. "You think I don't know what's going on upground? I know you've joined forces with the birds!"

Shade looked at Marina in alarm. What was he talking about?

"Yes, that's right," said the prince, catching their look. "You're surprised at how much I know. I have reports. I'm kept abreast of everything."

He looked around at the assembled rats, as if daring them to disagree.

"The king himself sends messengers to me!" His eyes snapped back to Shade and Marina. "And I know about the vicious attacks you and your bird allies have been making at night. You've killed rats, and our squirrel and mice cousins too."

With a sickening jolt, Shade understood. He remembered the rats Goth had killed. How many, he couldn't say. And who knew how many more since they'd separated. The prince thought Goth and Throbb were birds . . .

"Black owls, isn't it?" said Prince Remus, saliva flying from his mouth. He looked up as if he expected one of them to plunge from overhead. "The black owls are your allies. Speak!"

Shade didn't know what to say. The idea of bats allied with owls was crazy. It was impossible. But telling the truth was pointless. The prince would never believe him, and he didn't want to risk making him angrier than he already was.

"Yes, Your Highness," said Shade. "The black owls have joined forces with a group of jungle bats."

From the corner of his eye he saw Marina glance quickly at him, but wouldn't turn to meet her gaze.

"Jungle bats?" Remus jerked forward. He looked to the rats assembled around him, then to his chief guard. "Why haven't I heard about these jungle bats? How am I supposed to run my kingdom when no one informs me?"

"That's why we've come to you, Your Highness," Shade told him. He was inventing furiously, praying the words would keep flowing into his head. "We wanted to let you know exactly what was going on. These bats come from the jungle, and have betrayed the rest of us by siding with the owls against bats and rats alike."

"Jungle bats . . ." muttered Prince Remus to himself, as if he still couldn't understand how he hadn't heard about this. He looked at Shade suspiciously.

"Who sent you?"

Before he could form a reply, Marina spoke. "The great bat elders of the mountain colonies," she told him. "You're well known in our kingdoms. Everyone knows the name of Prince Remus."

"Of course they do," the rat prince said haughtily. "Of course they know me. And fear me, yes, fear me and the might of my kingdom . . ."

He paused and stared hard at Shade, and his eyes glinted with an intelligence Shade hadn't seen before.

"It's very good of you bats to warn me."

Shade nodded, biding his time.

"Very generous of you," the prince said softly.

"We didn't want there to be any misunderstanding." Shade could feel a trickle of cold sweat slither through his fur. "These jungle bats are traitors. Our colonies want to keep the peace with you."

The prince still stared at him, as if trying to bore into his head. Shade didn't dare look away.

"You're lying."

"No, Your Highness—"

"This is a trap, isn't it. You're planning a surprise attack. Look around you! Do you see the number of soldiers I have here? Do you think you're the only ones with powerful friends? I am known to the king! I can ask for his help! I can summon our beast allies. Wild dogs, raccoons. Even the wolves will come to the aid of Prince Remus! We can wipe you out!"

"Your Highness, please—" It was spinning apart.

"I want to know the position of your forces."

"I don't know—"

Shade's head was pushed down into the mud, brown ooze flooding up his nostrils. He struggled wildly, but the guard's grip held him until he thought his chest would burst. He came up gagging.

"Who sent you?" demanded the prince.

"I told you, the great elders of—"

The prince shook his head. "Take them to the drain," he told the guards, "and drown them."

"Fly!" Shade shouted at Marina, and spread his wings. But the rat guards fastened their jaws around his forearm, and he knew if he tried to lift off, his arm would be ripped from its socket. Another guard had Marina's wing tip in his mouth, ready to tear. Shade sank back down into the mud.

"Take them away!" shouted the prince.

"Bring them to me first!"

The terrible shrieking voice issued from one of the many grates high in the wall. A dreadful silence fell over the mob in the palace courtyard, and Shade could tell they were all afraid of that voice. And that made him afraid too. He looked at the prince, and even he seemed taken aback.

"I want to see them, Remus!" came the voice again.

Shade tried to get a fix on it, and high up in the wall, he caught a blur of silvery movement from behind a set of metal bars. What was up there? What kind of animal made a noise like that?

He couldn't decide which was worse—being drowned, or being taken to the owner of that unearthly voice.

"Take them," Prince Remus snapped at the guards, and then smiled grimly. "Let him do what he will. And then bring them back to me. If they're still alive."

The rat guards led them up a series of steeply sloping tunnels. Hollowed out by rats rather than Humans, they were muddy and lumpy, globs of filth dropping from the ceiling. Shade peered down the innumerable side passages, trying desperately to think of an escape plan. He was exhausted already by the long climb, his breath ragged, limbs aching. There was no way they could outrun the rats, not in this muck.

"Here!" the chief guard said, stopping them beside a large stone.

Several of the rats put their shoulders to the stone and pushed. Slowly it slid across the mud, revealing a low opening in the oozing wall. Shade did not want to look inside. Even the guards seemed ill at ease, their whiskers twitching, casting worried glances at the chief.

"Take them in," the chief instructed two of the rats.

"I want them alone!" the shrill, unearthly voice cried from the darkness.

The chief guard nodded, relieved, and the rats began prodding Shade and Marina toward the entrance. Shade tried to dig his claws in, but the mud offered no support, and he merely slid on his belly through the opening, Marina right behind.

"Roll back the stone!" the voice instructed.

As the stone was quickly being pushed back into place, Shade fearfully cast his sonic eye around the chamber. At one end he could see the grate that overlooked the rat palace. And sprawled to one side was the owner of the voice. It was a rat, large and hunched, not as fat as Prince Remus, but imposing nonetheless. Shade was almost relieved. He didn't know quite what he'd imagined, but it was certainly worse than this.

"I've waited a long time for an opportunity like this," said the rat hungrily, shifting himself onto his feet and sniffing forward a little.

Shade stiffened, drawing closer to Marina. He could feel his heart pounding, his muscles tightening, and he knew there was still some fight left in him.

"Very clever what you did down there," the rat said. "I thought you were going to get away with it. Playing on the prince's paranoia, and flattering him at the same time. Very nicely done. I'm amazed he caught on, really."

Shade said nothing, watching the rat, ready to fight if he should suddenly lunge. He didn't sound like the other rats. He sounded . . . that was it . . . almost like a bat.

"His kingdom's in ruins," the rat went on. "He has almost no idea what's going on upground, because his messengers are unreliable, and his guards are forever deserting him to go to better kingdoms. The king despises him and tells him nothing. He lives in constant fear of attack. From birds, from bats. He's even afraid of me. And I'm his brother. My name's Romulus."

If he was the prince's brother, thought Shade, what was he doing sealed behind a stone like some sort of monster.

"I can see you're confused," Romulus said. "You see, the rumor is, I'm insane." He giggled heartily. "I'm not fit to rule. I'm a freak. That's what Remus tells everyone. So I'm kept up here, out of sight, out of the way. I'm the oldest, and by rights I should be prince. And the only way Remus could get power was by imprisoning me, and spreading stories about me."

The rat took another few steps closer, and Shade instinctively lowered his head, bared his teeth, and hissed.

Romulus jerked back in alarm. "I don't want to eat you!" he whispered indignantly. "Is that what you thought?"

"It did occur to us," Marina muttered.

"Why did you bring us here?" Shade demanded. He didn't know what to make of this strange rat. He glanced at the stone barrier, knowing that on the other side the guards were waiting to take them to the drain—if they came out alive.

"Don't worry about them," Romulus told him. "They can't hear a thing. And they don't dare disturb me." He paused. "I know you're not spies."

"You do?"

"I know why you came down here. You were being hunted."

"How did you know?" Marina asked.

"I saw it! I saw the two giant bats who were chasing you. I was upside in the Humans' town when you flew down into the grate. I've seen the world, you know, believe it or not." He gestured around the dank chamber. "I've not spent my whole life here. But it's been a long time since anything this exciting has happened, I can tell you. And I never thought I'd get a chance to see you up close."

"What do you mean?" Shade asked.

"Bats. I've seen quite a few from a distance, but never close enough." His whiskers twitched excitedly. "I have a special interest in bats, and . . . may I see your wings?"

Shade was beginning to wonder if Romulus was crazy after all.

"I'll stay back here, I promise."

Shade looked doubtfully at Marina, but for some reason he wasn't afraid of Romulus anymore. He didn't understand why the rat wanted to see his wings, but there was an innocent excitement in his eyes, a burning curiosity, which made Shade trust him.

"All right," he said. He unfurled his wings.

Romulus stayed where he was, peering intently at the taut leather. "Could you lift them just a . . . yes, thank you . . . and now angle them . . . ah . . . yes . . . ," he said, grunting to himself, muttering words Shade couldn't make out. After a few minutes he nodded. "Thank you," he said. "You can't know how important this is to me. Maybe if I showed you. Look."

Now he lay down in the mud and stretched out his arms and legs as far as they would go. Shade gasped. For although this creature was clearly a rat, there were long webs of skin between his arms and hind legs—almost the same leathery material bat wings were made of. More folds of skin stretched between his feet and stubby tail. And, if you looked closely, there were even flaps of membrane between his neck and arms.

"Wings," Shade breathed in amazement.

"You can see why my brother thinks of me as a freak," Romulus said. "To him, I'm scarcely a rat at all."

Shade turned to Marina. "I had a feeling . . . on the raft I was looking at the guards and I thought, really, with wings, we'd look sort of the same!" And maybe that explained Romulus's voice too, that strange batlike shriek of his.

"We're related, I think," said Romulus. "I think that millions of years back we were the same creature."

He rustled the taut flaps of skin between his arms and legs. "And I think these are memories, lost secrets that just happened to find their way out in me. I've spent a lot of time upside, years of my life studying this." He stood. "Of course, I could be wrong. It's just a theory. And not a popular one in my brother's court, as you might imagine. If he didn't think I was crazy, I'm sure he'd have drowned me years ago. Being a freak has its benefits, I can assure you."

Shade was silent for a moment, trying to digest all this. To think they could be related to rats.

"Strange we should now be enemies, isn't it?" said Romulus.

Shade nodded. "Those big bats you saw. The ones chasing us. They really are from the jungle. They're the ones who've been killing rats. We can't stop them."

"Somebody must," said Romulus, "before they start a war between all the creatures."

"Might be too late for that," said Marina. "Anyway, we've got enough to worry about. How are we going to get out of here?"

"That," said Romulus with a grin, "is easily taken care of."

He shuffled to a wall of his chamber and began to dig through the mud with his front claws, kicking out a pile behind him. After a few minutes he'd exposed a narrow tunnel.

"How else do you think I get upside so frequently?" he said. "Follow this. It should take you to the outskirts of the Humans' town. You'll have to crawl, I'm afraid. A little undignified, perhaps, for bats, but a small price to pay for your lives. My brother is not known for his mercy."

"What will you tell him?" Shade asked.

"I'll tell him I ate you both, right down to the marrow."

"Thank you," said Shade.

"Maybe," said Romulus, "the three of us will meet again one day, under better circumstances."

# CAPTURE

He scrambled after Marina through the airless tunnel, up and up and up, his claws plunging deep into the mud with every step. The tunnel widened and narrowed erratically, twisting into steep spirals. They had to flatten themselves, belly down, inching their bodies forward. Twice they had to dig their way through cave-ins, Shade fearing all the while they would be buried alive. His sound sight was practically useless in such close quarters. He moved like a blind thing, nudging ahead by feel. Every so often the tunnel seemed to run close to others, and he could hear the sound of rat claws on stone and pipe, sometimes muffled voices. He and Marina would freeze, not daring to breathe, waiting for the noises to go away. He was terrified that at any moment rat snouts would burst through the muddy walls, snapping.

Finally, the blackness began to soften and Shade could smell something above the choking stench of mud. Fresh air, just a hint, and then it was quickly overpowered by something else not so pleasant.

"What is that?" Marina asked in disgust.

Eager to get above ground, they sped up anyway, and surfaced inside a huge mound of stinking Human garbage. Shade nearly gagged, not wanting to touch any of it. He made his body as small as possible as he cast around for a way out. He spotted a channel, which Romulus had burrowed through the garbage, and hurriedly scuttled through it.

The night sky opened above them. Shade spread his wings joyfully and lifted up into it. He rose with Marina at his side, and watched with glee as the Human garbage and the mud and rats dropped farther and farther below him. He was rising away from it all, and how wonderful to finally be back in the night, his true element.

"I thought we'd had it down there," said Marina. "I really couldn't see a way out."

"Romulus," Shade said, turning to Marina, "he was our unexpected ally, wasn't he? Just like Zephyr said."

Marina looked at him curiously, then nodded. "Yeah, I think maybe you're right. Who'd have thought a rat would save our lives?"

Shade could now see the garbage dump, and the Humans' town off to one side, and then the forests stretching out before them, beckoning. His senses were automatically checking the sky for signs of Goth and Throbb.

"You think they're still looking for us?" he asked Marina.

"They don't give up easy, that's for sure."

Maybe they'd finally decided to head south on their own. Maybe they'd been run over by one of those Human machines on the road. There was certainly no sign of them now.

The ground was silver with snow, and it was still bitterly cold, but nothing like the mountain peaks. Shade realized how far south they must have traveled now. How many wingbeats, he wondered, and how many more to go?

"Which way?" Marina asked him.

Shade closed his eyes and summoned his mother's map. He started at the beginning, to make sure he didn't miss anything. With a lump in his throat he saw Tree Haven disappearing into the distance. The lighthouse, flashing. And then the rocky coastline, and the terrible ocean spreading away into blackness. Then came the city's dazzling lights, and the cathedral tower, the metal cross, and their guiding star. Ice, and the stone wolf ears in the mountain range. And then this—

Forest sweeping past beneath him. Snaking through the trees was a calm, glassy river. He was flying along the river now, downstream, following its every curve. And then, a sound, a low rumbling, growing, growing.

The river sped up, frothing, leaping—and all the while, this strange roar building. He thought of the sea, the crash of the waves on the shore.

And—

His last image was of this broad torrent crashing between rocky banks, sending up a spray. Then he was plunging toward the water, headfirst it seemed, his stomach lurching.

He tried to explain it to Marina.

"I got the river part," she said. "But I'm not sure about the last bit. We're supposed to go into the water? Your colony sure likes riddles, Shade, that's all I can say."

"At least we know where we're headed. Hibernaculum must be somewhere nearby. We're almost there, Marina. Maybe not more than a couple nights' flying."

He felt a surge of strength. They'd come so far. They'd make it after all. He angled his wings and streaked toward the forest, searching for the river.

And then the whole sky suddenly came unstuck and dropped down, pounding all his senses from him.

He woke in darkness, not knowing where he was, or what had happened. His last memory was of being wrapped in the suffocating weight of the night. He blinked. Where was he? There were no stars, no moon. He pricked up his ears, hoping for a silvery picture of the world in his mind's eye. But from all sides, his echoes bounced back at him hard.

He was trapped in some tiny space, so tight he couldn't even unfurl his wings.

Suddenly he was aware of a thick, unpleasant smell, and a fast, rhythmic thudding. At first he thought this was his own racing heart. Then, in horror, he realized it was someone else's heart, very, very close.

All around him, the walls seemed to shudder in time with the beats. It was as if—

He was inside a living thing.

With a terrible calmness, the answer came to him.

You've been eaten.

You're inside the stomach of some huge animal.

Panic exploded through him and he started to struggle against the leathery walls. Let me out, let me out! The walls contracted even tighter, threatening to squeeze the air out of him altogether. He stopped, gasping and sweating.

The walls shuddered and loosened slightly. Fresh air snaked in and Shade breathed hungrily. In the pale light he could now see the walls were made of some kind of leathery material . . . a bat's wing.

He cried out as the wing pulled back suddenly and Goth's huge head loomed over him.

"Nothing broken, I hope."

"Where's Marina?" Shade gulped.

"Oh, we've got her too."

They were at the back of a shallow cave. Throbb, crouched nearby, slowly unfolded his right wing, and Marina emerged, gasping for air. Shade met her eyes. He crawled warily out from under Goth's wing, and was sickened by what he saw.

Before, the cannibal bat had only the single black band. But now his forearms, and even his hind legs, were festooned with glimmering silver rings. Throbb too was decorated, though not nearly as lavishly as his companion. Shade now understood the terrible metallic whistling that had followed them through the night skies.

"You killed them, didn't you," croaked Shade.

"You led us right to them, really."

Shade turned to Marina, watching her face. She looked like she was going to be sick. All those bats, all they'd hoped for, gone forever now.

"Don't worry, we didn't eat them all," said Goth. "There's only so much bat even I can stomach."

"You're a monster," Marina hissed.

"They thought the same," Goth said. "Kept calling out to the Humans to help them. Seemed to think they were even going to turn *into* Humans. Pathetic. You're not still waiting for them are you?" he asked her mockingly. "I'd have thought your last encounter with Humans was proof enough they don't care about you."

"I wish they'd killed you," Marina said.

"They nearly did. I ripped the dart out just in time." He looked at Shade. "I need the rest of your sound map."

Shade's throat tightened. "Why?"

"I want to go to Hibernaculum and meet Frieda, and all the other Silverwings."

"I've forgotten the rest."

"You're lying."

"No. We're lost."

Goth looked at Throbb and nodded. Throbb opened his jaws and closed them lightly over Marina's head.

"Tell me how to get there, Shade."

He looked at Marina, could see a trickle of Throbb's saliva drip down onto her face. She winced in disgust, breathing fast and shallow. The teeth closed a little more, pressing into her.

"It's a river!" Shade shouted. "Through the forest. A river, and we're supposed to follow it."

"Where to?"

"I don't know, I really don't. We can't figure it out. The picture doesn't make sense."

Goth stared hard at him. "You'll have to figure it out, won't you."

He nodded.

Goth jerked his head at Throbb. "Let her go for now. Shade has some thinking to do."

"They'll fight you," he said fiercely. "There're thousands of us there."

"Show me this river. We've wasted enough time."

Goth and Throbb flanked them tightly, wing tip to wing tip. Shade knew there was no escape. If they tried to bolt, the big bats could overtake them in a second.

It wasn't long before he heard the soft sound of running water, and he felt sick. He locked onto it and, skimming the trees, brought them out over the river.

"How far is it?" Throbb asked, shivering.

"Maybe two nights, maybe more. I'll know when we hit the landmark."

"I hope you know what you're doing," Goth hissed at him. "If you're trying to trick us, think of your friend Marina."

They flew in silence for an hour, following the curves of the river. His colony. He knew they were close, and his heart ached. He wanted to sleep. He wanted to be warm. He wanted to surrender all his problems. After an hour the horizon started to glow.

"I'm hungry," Marina said. "We haven't eaten for a long time."

It was true, Shade realized. He hadn't even noticed the yawning pit in his stomach.

Goth looked at them. "Yes, go eat some of your little insects, but stay within sight along the river. We'll be watching."

With the two huge bats circling overhead, Shade and Marina searched joylessly for insect eggs and snow fleas, not daring to speak.

"They're going to kill us, you know."

He nodded, remembering Zephyr's words. Powerful agents were searching for Hibernaculum. But who would get there first?

"As soon as they know how to get there," Marina said, "they won't need us anymore. They'll eat us."

And what would they do to his colony? Could the Silverwings fight Goth and Throbb? The males would be there. Surely, all together, they could beat the cannibal bats, no matter how powerful they were.

But . . .

What if Goth and Throbb didn't come fighting? Coldness seeped through him. What if they came to the colony the same way they'd come to him? Peacefully. Helpfully. What if the Silverwings trusted them, and let them hibernate with them? They'd be eaten in their sleep. One after another, all through the winter. And no one would wake up to notice until it was too late.

"What's that scar on Throbb's wing?" he asked Marina.

"Frostbite. I've seen it before. A bat got lost in an ice storm for a couple of nights. He lost his whole wing."

Shade started thinking. "Will that happen to Throbb?"

"Maybe. The tip looks pretty bad. It'll spread."

"Goth'll get it too."

"He's a bit bigger, but he can't take the cold either. Who knows, Shade. It might take weeks."

"If we take them off course, maybe, keep them in the cold . . ."

But how long could he risk that before Goth lost his patience, and killed them both? Goth was already suspicious. He didn't trust him. And how long could he and Marina stand the cold?

Goth plunged down toward them.

"That's enough," he said. "We need to find a roost."

Shade looked away as the two cannibals tore into the finch they'd brought back from their hunt.

They'd found a roost in the small hollow of a dead tree. It was cramped inside, and Goth and Throbb hunched across the opening, blocking it. Shade noticed that Throbb was shivering violently as he ate, rubbing his scabby wing against the rough insides of the tree. The finch's innards steamed.

"My eating habits still disgust you, I see," Goth said.

"You eat bats. It's unnatural."

"More unnatural than wanting to become Human?" Throbb laughed harshly as he chewed.

Goth snorted in disgust. "Those banded bats in the mountains, they made a religion of worshipping Humans instead of Zotz."

Zotz. The name, for some reason, sent a chill through Shade.

"You've never heard of him, have you?"

"No." And he didn't want to hear.

"Cama Zotz is the bat god. He created us, and everything around us, even this frozen wasteland you call home."

"No." Shade shook his head. "Nocturna created us and—"

"Why d'you even bother listening to him?" said Marina angrily. "He's a liar."

"Am I? Tell me then. Why would a bat god want his creatures to become something else? Zotz wants us to be powerful as we are. He doesn't want us to become Human."

"I don't even know if I believe that anyway," Shade said. "Maybe that's not what Nocturna means for us."

Goth smiled, and it was the kind of smile a mother gives a very young child.

"Nocturna doesn't exist."

Shade felt as if he'd been hit in the stomach.

"Or if she does exist, she's next to powerless. Look at her creatures. Cowering from everything in the sky and on the ground. Zotz is all powerful. Look at me!" He flared his mighty wings, bared his teeth, hunched his muscular shoulders. "This is what power is. I fear no creature. I eat them. Rat, owl, bat. Not even the Humans can hurt me."

Shade felt faint, but he couldn't tear his gaze away from Goth.

"You eat insects. They're living creatures, they just happen to be smaller than you. And weaker. But that doesn't stop you, does it? The real reason you don't eat like us is simple. You *can't*. You're too small. Meat is where the power is. When I eat another bat, I take in the strength of that bat, I take that bat's power and make it my own. And I grow. You've been starving yourselves on insects up here in the north. It's you who's unnatural. Not me."

Shade's head swirled with doubts. He'd heard so many stories now, from Frieda, from Zephyr, from Scirocco, and now from Goth. How was he supposed to know what was right and wrong? He was a runt, puny and powerless. But all bats were puny compared to these giants. How could they ever hope to beat the owls, beat the rats, win back the sun. He was powerless to even help his own colony, to keep Silverwings safe from Goth and Throbb.

"Maybe you're right," he said to Goth wearily.

Marina looked at him, startled. "Shade—"

"No, really, Marina, what if they're right, and this is how it is. There're bats and owls and rats and Humans, and the strongest wins, and it's as simple as that. The only thing is power."

"To you, maybe," said Marina disdainfully. "I should've known. All this curiosity of yours about the bands, and beating the owls, and getting back into the sun—all you care about is being big and important."

"You're no different," he shot back.

"What?"

"You wanted it just as much as me. You got your band, and you wanted to believe you were special too. That it meant something and you were better than all the other Brightwings. It's the same thing."

"At least I don't want to be like these two," she said with icy coldness. "I forgot. It's what you want more than anything, isn't it?"

Shade said nothing, but he caught Goth's eye, and saw a smile flicker across his mouth.

"You could grow, Shade," Goth said to him. He ripped a hunk of bird meat off the bone and held it out to him in his teeth. To Shade's surprise, his mouth began to water. They hadn't let him feed enough on insects, and food had been scarce the past few nights in the mountains. He was so hungry. What would it taste like? He wondered if it really would make him grow, so he could shrug off his runt's body once and for all.

"What can a taste hurt?" said Goth. "The birds are no friends of yours. Try it, Shade."

"No," he said, glancing guiltily at Marina.

Goth laughed. "You're afraid, aren't you? Afraid you might like it!"

"No."

Goth tossed the meat down his own throat and gave a mocking laugh.

When he'd stripped the bird clean, Goth spread one of his wings. "You'll sleep under here," he told Shade. "To make sure you don't go anywhere. Throbb, take Marina."

Shade's nose wrinkled in revulsion as he crept under Goth's wing, and it folded down over him, enclosing him in a fog of sweat and raw meat. He listened to Goth's huge heart pounding inside his chest, and fell asleep with dark thoughts gathering in his head like thunderclouds.

# BETRAYAL

"I want to go to the jungle with you."

Goth looked over at Shade, intrigued. They were flying side by side over the winding river. The water was running more quickly now, bubbling over rocks.

Ahead of them, Throbb shadowed Marina. She'd refused to fly next to Shade, hadn't even said a word to him this evening as they'd set out. Throbb, he noticed, had developed a strange, limping flight; he kept his wounded wing folded up so it slapped halfheartedly at the air. He didn't look healthy. His fur was greasy and matted, his eyes runny, and he shivered constantly now, even in flight.

"Why," Goth asked him, "do you want to go to the jungle?"

"I want to be like you. I want to be with bats who are powerful and who worship Zotz."

Goth laughed. "What about your beloved Nocturna?"

"She's powerless, you're right. I thought about it all through the day. The Promise is a lie. We'll spend our lives afraid of everything."

"And you're willing to abandon your own colony?"

"They won't be around much longer, will they? I know what you're planning. You're going to try to trick them into trusting you. Maybe it'll work, maybe not. If it does, then you'll eat them one by one through the winter as they sleep." He said it calmly, without emotion. "And I know you're planning on killing me before we get there."

"You're right."

"I don't care what you do with the others. Just take me back to the jungle with you."

"You really don't care if I eat your colony?" He seemed interested.

"They hate me. They blame me for getting the nursery roost burned down by the owls. And they never liked me even before that anyway. For a while I thought I could make it up to them, help them fight the owls. But they don't want anything to do with me. Why should I care about them?"

"Even your mother?"

He shrugged, his face hard. "She never came to look for me when I got lost—she just kept going and gave me up for dead. She thought I was more trouble than I was worth."

Goth looked at Marina.

"And her?"

Shade snorted bitterly. "She still thinks the Humans are going to come save us. You're right, it's pathetic, wanting to be something we're not. She just thinks I'm weak and greedy for power."

"Aren't you?"

"Yes." He looked Goth right in the eye. "I am greedy. I've spent my whole life as a runt, and I want to get bigger and stronger. I want you to show me how to hunt and fight."

Goth looked across the horizon thoughtfully.

"I don't trust you, Shade."

"You have to."

He snapped back, surprise in his eyes. "I don't think so. I could kill you right now."

"Then you'd freeze to death. You need me to get you

to Hibernaculum. You think this is the worst winter gets? This is just the beginning. Look at Throbb. He's got frostbite. In a couple of nights he probably won't be able to fly. Then he'll lose his wing. You'll get it too if you don't hurry. You don't have enough fur to protect you. You need a warm place for the winter. Fast. And you need me to help convince the Silverwings you're their friend."

Goth didn't look amused anymore.

"So that's the deal," Shade told him. "I take you to Hibernaculum, and you take me to the jungle."

The cannibal bat was silent a moment. Then he nodded.

"You have a deal, little bat."

Maybe he'd underestimated Shade.

From the corner of his eye, Goth watched the little bat in flight. There certainly wasn't much to him now, but that could be changed . . . with meat he would grow.

Shade was right. He did need him. If they didn't reach Hibernaculum soon, Throbb would certainly die. Not that Goth cared about that feeble, flying carcass. But even he was starting to feel an unpleasant numbness in his wing tips. He needed warmth.

And Shade might be more use to him alive than dead. Maybe he could help him convince the Silverwings to come down to the jungle. He'd make it worth Shade's while. He could give him special privileges. And he'd certainly be a more useful companion than Throbb. He was sharp-witted, this runt. He might not be much of a fighter, yet, but there was intelligence, and hunger, in his eyes. He did want power, and Goth had to respect that.

Was he really willing to sacrifice his own kind, and Marina too? At first he'd been doubtful, but after a while, he began to believe Shade was telling the truth. The little runt was smart, after all.

He'd seen the truth.

"That's it," Shade said suddenly to Goth. "The last

landmark." He pointed with his wing tip toward a tall hill on the western horizon.

Goth looked. "You never said anything about a hill."

"But I knew I'd remember when I saw it. I just forgot that part of my mother's map. We leave the river and go over the big hill, and it shouldn't be much farther than that. Don't think so, anyway."

He judged the distance in his head. He felt sick. Another night's flight, maybe two, would bring them to that hill.

"Good," said Goth. "This way!" he shouted to Throbb and Marina. "Shade's decided to cooperate after all."

Marina shot a look back at him over her wing. He met her eyes for only a moment, long enough to see the disgust in them. Then he had to look away.

"It's getting brighter," Goth said. "We'll feed here and find a roost for the day. Stay in the clearing where we can see you."

Shade fluttered cautiously down to the treetops. They hadn't encountered any owls or other birds lately, but he still kept a sharp eye and ear out for them.

"What're you doing?" Marina hissed, darting in front of him.

"What does it matter," he said coldly.

He could see Goth circling low overhead, watching, and he knew how good his hearing was.

"You're not really leading them to Hibernaculum."

He said nothing.

"Tell me if you are, because I'll make a break for it on my own."

"I wouldn't."

"No?"

"They'll catch you."

"How could you do this? To your own colony? To me?"

He looked at her hard, wanting to speak more than anything. But he couldn't. She flew away from him, to feed by herself.

His heart felt heavy as stone. He ate without even noticing, searching in the places Marina had taught him. He fluttered past a bush, looking for cocoons, and that's when he saw the leaves. He stared at them for a long time. Something familiar about them. Yes, he recognized the shape, the dark-veined texture. But where . . . ?

In the cathedral spire.

Zephyr had mulched that leaf up and drizzled it into his mouth. The leaf that had made him sleep.

Shade almost whimpered in gratitude.

He looked carefully up at Goth and Throbb. They had settled on a treetop to watch over him and Marina. Shade landed on the bush, still in plain view. He found a sac of cricket eggs and ate it hungrily. While chewing, he slowly reached over with one claw and tore a dark-veined leaf off its twig. Slowly he crumpled it deep under his wing, in a fold tight against his body.

He glanced up at the two cannibals. They didn't seem to have noticed. Goth was preening himself, preparing for a hunt.

Shade flew from the bush and continued feeding.

Goth brought a bat back to the cave and tore into it hungrily. His stomach churning, Shade saw that it was a Brightwing. Marina stared hard at the two cannibals, eyes blazing.

"Be grateful I found this straggler," Goth told her, "or it might be you getting eaten right now."

Shade took a slow, deep breath. "I'd like some."

Goth and Throbb looked over at him.

"Oh, ho!" crowed Goth. "The little one has developed an appetite for meat after all."

"There's not enough for him tonight," said Throbb. "Let him catch his own meat."

"Don't be so ungenerous, Throbb," said Goth. "We have a convert of Zotz in our midst."

From the corner of his eye Shade caught Marina staring at him in disbelief.

"Go ahead, have your fill," said Goth.

Shade slowly stepped toward the carcass, willing himself not to lose courage at the last moment. He turned his back to Goth and Throbb as he bent over the half-devoured bat. He didn't want them to see his face.

Over the last few minutes he'd been chewing the leaf, so slowly nobody had noticed. He'd been extremely careful. He hadn't swallowed so much as a single drop. He held it in one pouch of his mouth, ground up and mixed with his saliva into a clear potion.

Now, leaning over the body of the bat, he pretended to eat, dipping his teeth down. But he didn't eat, he simply let the leaf's liquid dribble silently over the carcass. A bit here, a bit there. He was lucky the liquid had no smell, and not much of a taste either—nothing to alert the two cannibals to its presence.

"He's hardly eating at all!" whined Throbb, lurching closer to see what Shade was doing.

Quickly Shade closed his mouth.

"Eat!" growled Goth, batting him with an outstretched wing. "You said you wanted to eat. So eat!"

Shade still had a bit of the potion in his mouth. There was no getting around it now. He had to eat some of the bat. His stomach lurched as he bent down and took a delicate bite, letting the last of the liquid flow out of his mouth at the same moment.

The taste of the meat brought water to his eyes. He tried not to touch it with his tongue, or let it remain too long in his mouth. He swallowed, almost choking, revolted and horribly ashamed. He felt as if he'd done something unspeakably evil. He couldn't stop the tears from streaming over his nose and fur.

"You'll get used to it," said Goth. "You'll soon get so that you can hardly wait to kill again."

Throbb roughly shoved Shade out of the way and

began feeding on the carcass. Shade crawled slowly back toward Marina, but she moved away from him, just staring at him with a look of utter hatred.

"Traitor," she said, and turned her back on him. "I wish I'd never met you."

Sunlight burned outside the cave.

Tentatively, Shade shifted his body, just a little to see if Goth would notice. The cannibal's heavy breathing continued undisturbed. Slowly, Shade eased his shoulders out from beneath Goth's wing. Then his chest, and his own wings, pulled in as tight as he could manage. He was halfway out when Goth twitched. His broad wing contracted, dragging Shade in closer toward his rank, damp body.

Shade forced himself to go limp, waiting fearfully for a few moments. But Goth did not wake. He ground his teeth together in his sleep, a string of saliva dripping from his open mouth. Shade looked away in disgust and began to slide his body forward again. Almost there, almost there, just his tail and hind legs to get clear.

One of his wings knocked against Goth's forearm, jangling two of the metal bands against one another. It produced a clear chiming.

"Shade," Goth said.

Shade froze in horror, then slowly turned his head. One of Goth's eyes was wide open, staring straight at him. But he wasn't moving. His eye was dead, unfocused.

He's still asleep, thought Shade.

They continued to stare at each other, Shade motionless, waiting to see what would happen next.

"Go to sleep," Shade said softly.

And as if on cue, Goth's eye dropped shut and his breathing returned to normal.

With a slow forward pull of his shoulders, Shade wriggled clear of Goth's wing. He crept forward to where Throbb was sleeping his drugged sleep, his ugly head drooped awkwardly to one side. Carefully he lifted a flap of his right wing and poked Marina's head gently with his nose.

"Shhhhh," he said softly when she stirred and opened her eyes. "Not a sound."

She stared at him with the same cold loathing as last night, and he suddenly worried she might say something, make a sudden noise that would undo all he'd worked for.

"Trust me," was all he could say, in a whisper.

He helped her clear of Throbb's wing and they both crawled silently toward the cave opening. They squinted out into the light of day.

"Close your eyes," he told her.

They closed their eyes, opened their wings, and flew.

# THUNDERHEAD

Even with his eyes squeezed shut, an angry glow seeped painfully around the edges, dimming his sound sight. With Marina beside him, he circled quickly, taking his bearings from the treetops. Then he flew headlong, back the way they'd come the night before. He wanted to get as far away from Goth and Throbb as he could before they woke from their drugged sleep.

He was in the sun. In the light of day. No bat had been here for millions of years.

He could feel the heat of it on his wings, the fur of his back, and even in the cold winter day, it still felt glorious. It felt like victory.

"Why didn't they wake up?" Marina asked.

"I drugged them."

He quickly told her about the leaf, and how he had to pretend to eat the bat. And then he went farther back, and told her about his plan. How he wanted to make Goth trust him, and then lead them west, away from Hibernaculum, in the hopes the cannibals would freeze to death, or become so weak he and Marina could escape and outfly them.

"Oh, Shade," she said softly. "I'm sorry. I didn't know."

"I know. I wanted it to be convincing, that's all." He faltered. "You don't hate me, do you?" Those looks she'd given him were hard to forget.

"Of course I don't hate you! You've saved us!"

"Not yet."

He had no stars to guide him. He hoped he could remember their route; last night, as he'd veered away from the river, he'd been trying to find landmarks that he could lodge in his memory.

"Will it hurt us?" she asked. "The sun."

"Hasn't turned us to dust yet."

"But will it blind us?"

"I don't think so. Those were just stories they told newborns. But it might be too much at first. Take it slowly. And never look right at it."

Gradually as he flew, he'd been letting his eyelids loosen, rising up bit by bit. The urge to open them was far greater than he'd imagined. He wanted so urgently to see the light of day in all its glory.

He cracked his eyes open just a little more and—

He heard Marina's gasp of wonder.

"You see it?" he whispered.

"Yes."

It was the same world he'd beheld his whole life at night, but now, under the sun's glow, it was transformed. Strangely, it was not as sharp and clear as he'd imagined. The sunlight seemed to haze things over, where his echo vision had always given him the cleanest of images. But there was a dazzling beauty to this new world. Everything seemed lit from all sides, the trees, the bushes, the dead leaves, the snow, even the air. It had a depth and texture he'd never imagined. He'd never noticed the air before, how it absorbed the light. He could almost feel it with his eyes. Everything shone.

The world was beautiful, but painful. His eyes weren't ready for any more. He left them open just a crack.

"Let's go higher," he said. He wanted to get away from those trees, high into the sky where there'd be fewer birds. For all he knew, a sharp-eyed crow was watching from below. They wouldn't have much warning if one struck.

At night, his black wings and body made him blend in; now they made him an easy target. Marina was a little better off, with her bright, pale fur.

It was getting darker, big clouds scudding across the sun. And there was a wind too, with the unmistakable smell of lightning in it.

"Storm coming," said Marina.

Asleep in the cave, Goth curled his wings against his body. His nose twitched. Something was wrong. He extended his wing, tapping it along the ground. He grunted and, with great effort, slowly raised his heavy eyelids. Shade was gone.

"Throbb," he moaned, his throat clogged with sleep. He coughed, rousing himself. "Throbb!"

Throbb slept on, oblivious.

Furious, Goth staggered up and lunged across the cave, ramming Throbb with his snout, tipping his wings to peer beneath them.

"What?" cried Throbb in alarm.

"They're gone!"

"It's still day," said Throbb, squinting out the cave opening. "They can't be—"

"They're gone!" Goth roared again. He sniffed the ground for their scents. "But not long ago. Get up."

"Into the light?"

"Yes."

"But it's not safe."

With a quick twist, Goth fastened his jaws around Throbb's wing, letting his sharp teeth bounce up and down on the blisters. Throbb yowled.

"The winter's not safe," hissed Goth. "And if we don't find that cave of theirs, we'll freeze to death! And you'll go first."

"All right, yes," whimpered Throbb.

They lurched to the cave opening, and launched themselves into the day.

The wind came up behind them like a demon, but Shade was glad. It meant there would be fewer birds out. And most important, they were being blasted farther and farther away from the cannibal bats. He could tell by the change in temperature and light that the sky was sealed tight with clouds. Already it was hard to steer, and Shade wondered how long they could fly before taking shelter. Below, the ground swept past with alarming speed and he felt barely in control of his wings.

"How're you doing?" Marina shouted above the wind.

"Scared," he said bluntly.

"Me too."

"We should be back to the river soon." If I haven't made a mistake, he thought worriedly. He thought he'd picked out some familiar landmarks, but there were stretches of ground that seemed totally new to him. But a few thousand wingbeats later, the stretch of trees was broken by the winding line of the river.

"There it is!" Shade shouted excitedly.

And there was an owl, rising from the trees directly in front of them.

"Lawbreakers!" shrieked the owl.

He was being blown straight toward it, they both were, and Shade knew they wouldn't escape its claws. No time to veer off, no time to climb higher. And in that endless split second, he remembered the tiger moth he'd hunted so long ago at Tree Haven, how slow and helpless it seemed, but . . .

He didn't even know if it would work.

But it was his only chance.

He closed his eyes and sang a sound picture at the owl. He drew a dozen different bats in the air around them, some soaring higher, some rolling to the side, others plunging to the ground.

He saw the owl hesitate. Where were the real bats? It was working! He'd thrown it off. But the owl shook its head and its horrible eyes looked straight at them, claws ready to grab and tear.

Shade tried once more. Crying out, he shot out an echo picture of Goth, three-foot wings spread, claws extended, jaws screeching open . . .

The owl caught the picture and bellowed in terror, plummeting back down to the trees, not even daring to look back.

"What'd you do?" Marina exclaimed.

"A little trick I learned from a tiger moth," he said cockily. "I'll teach it to you sometime."

A faint metallic tinkle reached his ears, and then dissolved. His whole body tensed. He held his breath, hoping he'd imagined it, hoping for silence.

"Did you hear that?" Marina asked.

Shade's heart pumped furiously. He craned his neck around, strained with his eyes, but saw only a black wrinkle in the distance, then nothing, then two wrinkles, gone again. But he heard, clearer now, the familiar metallic whistle, riding on the wind.

"How far are they?" Marina said.

"Can't tell. But how'd they know which way we went?"

"They're not stupid. In a wind like this, there's only one way we *could* go."

"Should've chewed up more leaves!" he raged. "Why didn't I? It would've been so easy. There was a whole bush, I could've—"

"Shade," Marina said. "Up there."

Boiling up on the horizon was a towering thunderhead.

"We'll lose them in that," she said.

He broke through the cloud's underbelly and was tossed around like a leaf. Inside, he was nearly deafened by his own echoes, bouncing back at him from all sides. It was like being inside a tiny cave. His sound sight was useless. It wasn't much better than flying blind. He crashed on through the walls of the cloud, unable to see more than a few feet in front of his nose.

"Marina!" he called out, and his own voice echoed dully.

From out of the mist she streamed alongside him.

"I can't see a thing," she said.

"They won't either," said Shade. "Let's try to break through the top. Then we can circle back, drop below the cloud, and find the river again."

Together they spiraled clumsily higher through the inside of the thunderhead. They kept losing sight of each other in hills and valleys of black mist. It was getting darker inside, the air almost too thick to breathe.

"Does your fur feel funny?" Marina whispered.

Shade glanced at his chest. The hairs were tingling, standing up on end.

"What's it mean?" he asked.

The air suddenly smelled different, metallic. The inside of the thunderhead was lit up with a flash of lightning, blinding them for a moment. A clap of thunder knocked the wind out of Shade's chest.

"We'd better break through the top soon," he wheezed, "or we're going to get struck!"

They tilted their wings, flapped harder, and a pair of huge jaws thrust out of the wall of mist before them. Shade rolled to one side as Goth lunged, snapping, but missing them both. Goth banked sharply, spinning himself around for a second pass.

Shade streaked blind through the thunderhead, not knowing where he was going, or where Marina was now. Through a veil of cloud he saw a darkening shadow, growing larger, heading straight toward him. He dove but not fast enough. Throbb burst upon him, raking at his tail with his claws, and hauling him backward through the air.

Shade heard Throbb's jaws snap open, ready to take a bite, and he slammed his wings straight up, braking, and flipping backward over the cannibal bat. As he rolled, he took a swipe at Throbb's wounded wing, dragging his claws deep.

Throbb howled, and snapped his wing tight to his body, careening out of sight.

Shade hovered for a moment, trying to gather his wits. Go to the top, his instincts told him. That's where we were headed. Marina would go there too.

All at once the air stung his nostrils, his fur stood on end, and he shut his eyes just in time. The lightning bolt shot past him, so close he could feel its tremendous heat; then thunder hard on its heels, blinding him in both ears.

He could barely see, barely hear, and he was flying with all the speed he could muster. All he knew was the difference between up and down. For a moment he thought he'd broken clear, but it was just a weird bubble within the thunderhead, like a magical cavern floating in the sky.

A horrible cry pierced the cloud.

"Marina!" he shouted in panic. He was sure it was her. "Marina! Where are you?"

Goth plunged down on him, snatching him up in one of his claws, and piercing his wing in two places. But the cry of pain died in his throat when he saw the glinting, bloody object between Goth's teeth.

Marina's band.

Enraged, he tried to claw at Goth's eyes, but the cannibal bat held him away from his body, a harmless runt.

"Throbb," he called out, "we've got our guide back." He looked back at Shade. "Here's the new deal. You take us to Hibernaculum right now, or I'll rip your insides out."

Goth suddenly reeled over onto his back, slammed by Marina's bright body.

"Come on!" she yelled at Shade.

He twisted free of Goth's grip and raced toward her. Her forearm was bleeding badly. But before they could dive into the sea of cloud, Throbb swung in from the side, blocking their escape. Shade pulled back with Marina, hovering wildly, as Goth and Throbb closed in from either side, wings wide open to catch them.

The air tingled again, Shade's fur snapping up from his body. The metallic smell was almost overwhelming this time, and it seemed to be coming from Goth and Throbb. His eyes locked onto the metal bands that festooned their bodies. From the black cloud above, a whisker-thin filament of light jumped down and lightly touched one of the bands around Throbb's forearm. The light flicked from side to side playfully.

"Get back!" he shouted to Marina, closing his eyes tightly.

The lightning struck in two forks, and Shade watched with his echo vision as Throbb was turned to ashes in a split second. Goth seemed to swell to twice his normal size as the fork hit him, all his fur leaping up from his body, his wings rigid at his sides, stretching, stretching. And the smell, the most terrible smell of burning fur and flesh.

Then Goth was falling, spinning lifelessly down, his wings burning. He was blown off to one side and swallowed up in the tumultuous darkness of the thunderhead.

"The lightning—it must have been the metal bands! It hit the bands first!"

"I saw it," Marina panted. "Lucky Goth took mine."

He looked at her bloodied forearm with concern.

"It's okay, it's not broken," she said.

Together they glided slowly down through the clouds. Shade winced as air whistled painfully through the gashes Goth had left in his wings. They were free! They plunged through the bottom of the thunderhead and back into the open air.

On the ground Shade gathered up some dried leaves to press against Marina's wound.

"I think the bleeding's stopped," he said after a few minutes. "I could go look for that berry Zephyr used."

"But what about you?" she asked, staring at his wings. The membrane hung limp in two places.

"It's okay, I can still fly."

"I can too, then," she said determinedly, shaking the leaves off. "Let's finish what we started."

Goth's body lay sprawled across the branches, charred and tattered. Smoke wafted from his burned fur.

A curious magpie hopped closer, even though the smell was terrible. The bird wasn't even sure what kind of creature this was, the wings and body were so singed. Whatever it was, it was certainly dead. The magpie wondered what had happened. Maybe a collision with one of those Human cables slung across the countryside—it was windy enough today, easy enough to get blown into them. Then again, there'd been lightning.

The magpie caught a flash of metal on the creature's body. Some kind of sooty ring on the forearm. And look, there were more of them. He hopped closer. He'd never seen a head like that on a bird. What jaws! But his attention fixed back on the bands. That's what he wanted. If he could just tug them off.

The stench from the creature was truly overwhelming. He dipped down with his beak and plucked at the shiniest of the bands. It was fastened tight. Mesmerized by its sparkle, he darted down again for another try and pulled hard.

Goth's eyes and jaws snapped open simultaneously. The last thing the magpie ever saw was a double row of sharp teeth streaking toward him.

After feeding a little on the bird, Goth felt some of his strength return. Every movement was painful, but he was still alive.

Alive.

He was truly amazed: Zotz must have been protecting

him from that bolt of lightning. He wondered if he could still fly. Slowly he unfurled his wings. They were seared and scarred in places, melted by the lightning's heat. Still, he probably had enough wing surface to fly.

He rested, ate, rested some more. By midnight, he could wait no longer. He had to find out if he could fly.

Shrieking with pain, he spread his wings, tensed his battered muscles and flapped. He plummeted many feet before the air caught under his wings, and he soared upward.

He would return to his homeland. He would pray to Zotz. He would become strong again. And then one day he would return to this northern wasteland and take his revenge on Shade and all his colony—so help him Zotz.

# HIBERNACULUM

The river surged, boiling over boulders.

He'd been following it with Marina for hours now, hoping that something would click in his head, telling him, finally, how to get to Hibernaculum. It was twilight. The lively burble of the water was building and, in the distance, Shade heard a low rumbling, which reminded him unpleasantly of ocean waves. Louder and louder, the water coursing faster between the banks until—

The river ended.

Shade gasped as it simply fell away in a sheer wall, plunging hundreds of feet to crash at the shore of a lake. He circled, staring.

"Waterfall," Marina said. "I've seen one before. What do we do now?"

Shade had never seen such a thing. Roaring water falling straight down through the air. There was no more river, nothing more to follow . . . but in an instant he finally understood.

*This* was his mother's last landmark: a broad torrent of water crashing between rocky banks, sending up a spray and roaring. He'd just been thinking about it the wrong way around, sideways instead of up and down.

"We're here," he breathed, and then louder: "This is it!"

"It is?"

"This is Hibernaculum."

"Where?"

"Follow me."

He began a slow dive, straight for the waterfall.

"Have you flipped out, Shade?"

"Come on!"

Marina reluctantly trimmed her wings and followed him.

He could already feel the mist on his face. As he plunged closer, he saw that the waterfall wasn't really a solid wall at all. The water fell differently all the way across, in fine sheets here, twisting cords there, misty plumes, heavy torrents.

"Shade? What're you doing?"

And there, just what he was looking for. Like a knot-hole in Tree Haven: a tiny circular hole in the middle of an undulating curtain of water. He locked onto it with his sonic eye, making sure it didn't close up.

"Stay right behind me!" he shouted to Marina.

He soared straight for the waterfall, folded his wings tight, and shot into the hole. Water thundered deafeningly in his ears—or was it his heart?—and even before he was through, he knew what he would see on the other side.

He burst into a vast cave. Hundreds of Silverwings swirled in the air, and hundreds more hung from the walls and giant stalactites that plunged from the ceiling.

Hibernaculum.

The colony had doubled in size, swollen by all the males who joined the females at Stone Hold. He could feel the warmth pouring from their bodies.

"Hey!" he shouted jubilantly. "Hello!"

He flew in tight circles with Marina, overwhelmed, his eyes flicking through the cloud of bats, trying to see his mother, Frieda, any familiar face. All these new bats were staring at him in surprise, and he was instantly inundated with questions. "Where did you come from?" and "Were you flying in the daylight?" and "Are you crazy?" and then "Wait, that's the newborn lost in the storm!" and "It can't be!"

"Yes it is!" he called out. "It's me! Shade! I got lost. But I found you!"

"Shade?" His mother's voice pierced the din. "Shade!"

His heart leaped, and he locked onto her with his echo vision. He wanted to fly to her instantly, but he couldn't leave Marina by herself.

"Come on," he said to her. "Come meet my mother."

With Marina at his side, he went to Ariel. They swirled around one another in amazement and glee before roosting on a ledge. Shade pushed his face into her warm, fragrant fur. Her wings enfolded him.

"We thought you were dead!"

"No," he said happily. "I'm alive. Mom, this is Marina. I met her after I got lost in the storm. Without her I probably would be dead."

Marina had settled a little ways off, watching awkwardly. Ariel stretched out her wing to her. "Come closer," she said gently. "Thank you." She nuzzled the Brightwing in gratitude.

"Well, it worked both ways," Marina said. "We helped each other out."

Ariel turned back to Shade, shaking her head. "Tell me what—" she broke off, seeing the punctures in his wings. "You're hurt!"

"It's not bad, really."

"And you are too," she said to Marina, looking at her bloody forearm. "We need to have that tended to—"

"It's not important right now," Shade said impatiently. He was about to explode with words. "Mom, Cassiel's alive!"

Her eyes narrowed in disbelief. "But . . . how do you know?"

"Zephyr told us, the albino bat, you know, the Keeper of the Spire, in the city. He can see into the past and the future and—" He took a deep breath, let it out in a rush.

"Start from the beginning."

It was Frieda, fluttering down to roost beside them. "Welcome back, Shade."

"I made it!" he told her gleefully.

"So I see." The bat elder's eyes crinkled with a smile as she reached out and touched Shade's head. "And I'm sure you have a lot to tell."

Starting from the beginning was agony for Shade.

He wanted to keep leaping ahead; he wanted to say everything at once. But he forced himself to go slowly. His wings were spread flat, his wounds covered with soothing berry juice. It wasn't just Zephyr who knew about potions after all. Frieda had insisted on tending to their injuries before she allowed them to begin. And now, Shade and Marina told their story together, each filling in any incident or detail the other missed out.

The whole colony was listening, spellbound. Even though it was well past twilight, and they could have been out hunting, preparing for their big sleep, the Silverwings chose to stay and hear what this young Silverwing and his Brightwing friend had to say.

As he spoke Shade picked out Aurora, Lucretia, and Bathsheba, roosting above him, and to one side, the four male Silverwing elders, whose names he didn't even know. They were very old, their fur bristling with silver and gray and white, and they peered down at him intently. He had a flash memory of himself in the upper roost at Tree Haven, stammering and afraid, but this time he was too deep inside his story to feel nervous.

Finally, he and Marina were finished. He had no idea how long they'd been talking, but he felt spent, his mouth parched. Mercury, the elder's messenger, brought them a leaf covered with water from the waterfall. Shade drank gratefully.

"We were lucky," said Frieda. "We kept just ahead of

the owl's order to close the skies. If it had caught up with us . . ."

Shade thought of the slaughtered Brightwings and shuddered.

"Now there *will* be a war," said Bathsheba bitterly. "Thanks to these jungle bats." But her steely eyes were fixed on Shade, and he knew that she also blamed him somehow.

"The owls have been waiting for an excuse to wage war for centuries," said one of the male elders. "If Goth and Throbb hadn't appeared, they'd have invented some other excuse to close the skies."

Shade's spirits plunged. Only hours ago he'd felt elated as he'd shot through the waterfall and into Hibernaculum. Now he realized how serious their situation was.

"At least the winter will halt any fighting," said Aurora. "The owls will be hibernating soon."

"True, but when spring comes," said Bathsheba grimly, "the owls will wipe us off the face of the earth."

"When spring comes," said Frieda levelly, "we must go to all the bat colonies and explain what has happened. And we must send envoys to the bird and beast kingdoms, in the hopes of stopping this madness."

"If they listen," said Bathsheba.

"If they don't, we must fight!" said another of the male elders.

A ragged cheer went up from some of the Silverwings. But Shade saw his mother's face harden.

Frieda sighed wearily. She seemed suddenly very old. "If the birds and beasts don't listen, and are intent on war, then, yes, we must fight."

"What about Nocturna's Promise?" came a voice. A male bat lit from his roost and swirled through the air. Shade caught a flash of metal from his forearm. "Have we given up all hope that Nocturna, or the Humans, will help us?"

"Who is that?" Shade whispered to Frieda.

"His name's Icarus. He was a friend of your father's."

Shade's pulse quickened.

"Don't speak of Nocturna's Promise," roared Bathsheba. "It's brought nothing but misery to the bat kingdoms. Have you forgotten the rebellion of fifteen years ago?"

"But maybe this Scirocco was right," said Icarus. "Maybe we *are* meant to turn into Humans."

"Only some of us," Shade said quietly, but his voice carried through the entire cave. "If Scirocco's right, only the banded bats will transform. That means almost all of us get left out."

Marina turned to Frieda. "Have you heard anything about a human transformation?" she asked.

"Yes, a long time ago, but I could never believe it was true."

But what if it was, Shade thought, feeling sick. He saw Marina look at her wounded forearm. What if she'd had her chance at the light of day, and given it up forever? Her band was gone now. But did that count? She was given it by Humans, and it was taken away by bats, but maybe . . .

She met his anxious eyes and smiled. "Don't worry," she said. "If I'd stayed with Scirocco, I'd probably be dead like the others." In a louder voice, so the whole of Hibernaculum could hear, she said: "I don't believe it either."

"It seems no one knows what the bands mean, then," said Bathsheba scathingly.

"But we have to find out," said Shade. "My father might know." He turned to Icarus. "Do you know where he was going when he disappeared last spring?"

Icarus said nothing.

"I'm his son," Shade said. "And I want to find him. I want to know what the bands mean, and if the Humans are going to help us or not. We all have to know."

"The boy's right," said Frieda. "Icarus, you knew Cassiel well. If you know where he went, tell us."

"There was a Human building," Icarus said uneasily. "Hanael saw it from a distance last spring. He said it had strange metal masts on the roof. But when he went back for a second look he didn't return. Cassiel went next. He made me promise not to tell anyone, it was too dangerous."

"He's there," breathed Shade with utter certainty. "I've got to go!" He looked at his mother. "You understand, don't you?"

She nodded. "I'll go too," she said.

"You will?"

"And me," said Frieda. "I'm old, but this is one journey I intend to make before I die."

"This is absurd!" shouted Bathsheba.

"Count me in as well!" said Icarus.

"And me," said a second banded male.

"Me too," cried another bat, and Shade recognized Chinook's voice. But he had no time to call out a greeting because a small avalanche of voices had started and his eyes flicked around the cave in delight as each bat called out, male and female, young and old.

"Bathsheba," said Frieda, "I take it you will not be joining us."

"Certainly not," said the elder. "I have no desire to end my life yet."

Shade suddenly realized something. Marina hadn't said a word. He turned to her worriedly, and there was a wistfulness in her smile that made his throat clench.

"You made it, Shade," she said. "You got home."

"You're not leaving are you?"

"I wonder if my own colony would take me back. Now that my band's gone."

"But . . . do you really want to go back?"

She sounded exasperated. "Well, I mean, I've got to go somewhere, don't I?"

"No. You don't," Shade exclaimed. "You can stay right here with me! With us! Can't she, Frieda?"

"Of course she can," said the bat elder.

"Really?" said Marina. "You don't mind having a Brightwing around?"

"Silverwings!" Frieda cried. "Do we have a home for a bat who has distinguished herself by such daring, loyalty, and heroism?"

"Yes," said Ariel eagerly, "stay!" And her invitation was echoed by a dozen, and then hund.eds of Silverwings until the cave reverberated with the sound of bat wings clapping the air in approval.

"This is your new colony," Shade told her, "for as long as you want, that is."

"I'm coming with you, then," said Marina. "I'm coming to find your father. And the secret of the bands."

That night the Silverwings hunted near the waterfall, keeping a careful watch out for owls. But it was hard for Shade not to feel secure in the midst of hundreds of his fellow bats.

He'd convinced Frieda and the others they should leave right away. Some had wanted to wait until spring, but what if his father were in danger? What if he were dying? And now that winter had set in, the owls would start their own hibernation. It was the safest time to make the journey. After all, it was only two nights' flying. It was all Shade could do to keep from setting off this very moment. But even he could see he'd need a few days' rest, for his wing to heal, to regain his strength.

His mother had told him he'd grown. He was genuinely surprised. He'd stared at his outstretched wings, his chest and arms. He *did* look bigger. In fact, with Marina close by, he saw that he was the same size as her now, maybe even a little larger. He was still nowhere near as big as Chinook, but that didn't seem so important anymore.

Back inside Hibernaculum, his stomach full, he

roosted between Ariel and Marina, their wings folded over one another for extra warmth. He listened to the sound of the waterfall pouring past the mouth of the cave, keeping them all safe and hidden inside. He listened to the softer sound of the stalactites, drip dripping onto the cave floor. He listened to the sound of his mother's breathing, the rustle of Marina's wings.

He tried to sleep.

But his mind wouldn't let him. He thought of all that had happened to him. He'd been swept out to sea and had made friends with a banded Brightwing. He'd flown over a great Human city and learned to navigate by the stars. He'd crossed the snowy peaks of the world and crawled deep below its surface. He'd heard the past and future in a bat's wings, seen the light of day, and flown through thunder and lightning. And within two sunsets, he'd be starting on another journey, and maybe the greatest of all.

"Go to sleep, Shade," Marina whispered in his ear.

Yes, he thought, eyes closing at last. Sleep.

# AUTHOR'S NOTE

I have a friend who's a real bat aficionado. He knows quite a bit about bats, and he even builds "bat boxes" for them, little wooden homes you nail high up on trees. I suppose a bit of his enthusiasm rubbed off on me, because I started doing some reading about bats. Right away I was intrigued by the different folk stories from across the world, which described the genesis of bats, why they fly only at night, and how they relate to other animals. Are they birds? Or are they beasts? I quickly became fascinated by these creatures that, in European society anyway, have traditionally been objects of fear. Certainly, some species are terrifying to behold (more unsightly than any gargoyle I've ever seen), but others, like the ones we get in most of North America—and the ones who are the heroes of *Silverwing*—tend to be like handsome mice with wings.

I was struck by what remarkable animals bats are: They see only in black and white (but can see quite well, despite traditional assumptions that they're blind), and use sound as much as vision to navigate their world. They migrate like birds, and no one really knows how they can find their way on journeys as long as a thousand miles. Some bats have been known to cross oceans.

All this seemed to me such rich material for creating a new fantasy world, complete with its own original mythologies and forms of technology and magic. I liked the challenge of creating a black-and-white world (I don't mention a single color in the book), and describing a bat's sonic vision, and the song maps they use to migrate. I also liked the challenge of taking animals that many might consider "ugly" or "scary" and fashioning them into interesting, appealing characters. Many animals had already been written about, and most of these were reasonably cuddly: horses, mice, rabbits, pigs, even spiders. But would kids be able to identify with bats?

## Shade is back—and so is Goth!
## in

# *Sunwing*

## the sequel to *Silverwing*

In search of his father—and the secret of the bands that Humans have attached to some bats—Shade discovers a mysterious Human building which contains a vast forest. Home to thousands of bats, the indoor forest is warm as a summer night, teeming with insect food, and free from the deadly owls.

Paradise?

Shade and Marina, his banded Brightwing friend, aren't so sure. Where is Shade's father? And what happened to all the bats who have suddenly disappeared? In this thrilling sequel, Kenneth Oppel surpasses the excitement and poignancy of *Silverwing*, which *Smithsonian* magazine called, "a tour-de-force fantasy."

## Coming in Spring 2000

# *Sunwing*

## by Kenneth Oppel

### Simon & Schuster Books for Young Readers